Like Seabirds Flying Home

Books by Marguerite Murray

Like Seabirds Flying Home

by MARGUERITE MURRAY

A Jean Karl Book
Atheneum 1988 NEW YORK

Atheneum
Macmillan Publishing Company
866 Third Avenue, New York, NY 10022
Collier Macmillan Canada, Inc.
FIRST EDITION
Printed in USA

Library of Congress Cataloging-in-Publication Data
Murray, Marguerite.
Like seabirds flying home/by Marguerite Murray.—1st ed. p. cm.
"A Jean Karl book."
Summary: Fifteen-year-old Shelley's dying father brings their
small family to the Nova Scotia fishing village of his origin, where
she falls in love and finds it increasingly difficult to deal with
her rebellious, irresponsible mother.
ISBN 0-689-31459-0
[1. Nova Scotia—Fiction. 2. Family problems—Fiction.]
I. Title.
PZ7.M963Li 1988
[Fic]—dc19   88-4396 CIP AC
10 9 8 7 6 5 4 3 2 1

To our friends in Nova Scotia

Old Jaimie

*T*HERE *was the Ford again, parked in front of the Reedie place, the last house on Sentinel Head. Old Jaimie Wenloch was uneasy. He straightened from his hauling of feedbags and watched the man circle the house. Then he snorted.*

On fine days, and they were few enough this far north, the headland would reach out for unwary tourists, city folk dazzled by the surround of blue sea. The house was cheap. Bait it was, and this fellow was biting all right. From the old farmhouse that Jaimie used as his sheep barn, and even though it was some distance across the moor, he could see the man come back to lean against the car, as if he were studying the situation. Suddenly the man stood up, walked quickly around the Ford, opened the door, and drove off. Sentinel Head had him hooked. Jaimie snorted again, but he was even more uneasy.

1

It was the name that bothered him. Joyner. *News traveled fast in these remote fishing villages, and Jaimie had already heard that the man was dickering with the agent. The name Joyner set his thinking back fifty-sixty years. He sighed and looked toward the winding path that led upward to the peak, land's end. He ought to follow the path; it was time to count his flock from that high place. But he was too old, too tired. He could no longer stand in the face of the wind. The sea, thundering on the rocks below him, no longer pleased him either, but mocked instead his growing weakness. Jaimie shook his head, scolding himself for the idea. He'd been a fisherman in his youth. He'd lived too long by the sea; he'd learned too many of its lessons over the years to think that the sea cared. It didn't care that his fence was in bad shape, or him either.*

Summer was almost over, and he still hadn't mended the fence. The last storm had done a lot of damage. He glanced seaward. There would be more storms, more damage, more worry. His mind returned to the man in the Ford. If the name Joyner meant anything at all, he would have to deal with it. It had taken all these years to put the war and his losses to rest: Why stir them up now? He wished the name had been anything but Joyner.

Chapter 1

ONCE AGAIN THE FORD PULLED UP TO THE REEDIE place, and this time Shelley Joyner crawled out of the clutter in the back of the car, leaving her parents motionless in the front seat. She stood in the road and looked at the old blind house before her, what she could see of its boarded-up front windows and salt-bleached shingles, for it hastily folded the fog about itself and retreated, ashamed. For a moment Shelley was too stunned to speak, and then a sob—just one—constricted her throat and forced its way out.

"Oh no, Vernon!" Her lips merely formed the words. Only the sob had escaped. "No!" She glanced at her parents. Catherine's sharp profile, rock carved, looked straight ahead into the fog. No compromise there, no accommodation to this place. Beyond at the wheel, Vernon sat indistinct, as unspecific as the fog itself. How *had* he got hooked into buying this awful place? Shelley ran her jacket sleeve across her eyes. Once. Then she straightened, as she always did. Over and over, after each disaster. And she wasn't going to give up now, no matter what.

Just the same, she'd waited all her life for this moment. She'd endured a succession of dismal flats and duplexes, waiting patiently—well, *mostly* patiently—for a true home, a Joyner place, and Vernon had promised it at last. A house by the sea. And *look* at it! Or at least try. The house reappeared for a second, then disappeared again. Wouldn't you think Vernon, for once, could have done it right?

"Better get out." Shelley addressed the two zombies on the front seat. They turned their faces toward her but made no move, either of them, to follow her advice. Shelley leaned for a moment against the car, waiting.

She'd been too eager to leave New Hope (Shelley called it No-Hope), the factory town where Vernon had worked forever. Until just two weeks ago, that is, when he'd retired. Without warning. On disability. She should have checked him! He was so plodding, so, well, penny pinching, so *reliable*, she corrected herself. She should have been suspicious right away of this decision to move—and so far away. Why—and how—had he found this faceless dot on the map, Sentinel Head, and this old dejected house? So what if he could afford it, if the air was better, if they would live by the sea? Had he for a moment considered Catherine? Or her?

It was still summer, late August, to be exact, but the clammy cold was reaching for her. No need to invite it in. Shelley zipped her jacket up to the neck, and hugged her arms tightly across her chest.

They'd crossed Nova Scotia from the Fundy side, and it had taken them forever. She'd rolled the car window down once to get a breath of air against Catherine's endless cigarettes, and she'd heard the ocean and even smelled it, but everything was so fogged in that she still hadn't seen the water. As they drove farther out onto the headland, the fog had

4

thickened even more, the houses had died away, the spruce trees had become sparser and sparser. Finally they must have driven beyond a marine timberline because the trees stopped altogether. Even the asphalt road had given way, first to gravel and then to dirt. SENTINEL HEAD: End of the World.

Shelley tightened her jaw and breathed in a lungful of fog. Whatever Vernon had gotten them into, there was no point in the two of them just sitting there. She opened the front door of the car. "Come on," she coaxed.

Inside, the house was even worse, if possible, than outside. It smelled of dry rot or at least disuse, as if it hadn't had a breath of sea air for a long time. The naked light bulb that Vernon turned on discovered their furniture huddled in the shadows of the living room. Shelley swallowed another sob. It was absolutely the end of the line.

It had all been so unexpected, Vernon coming home and quietly placing his lunch bucket on the table for the nth and last time, and the next day, without explanation and without either Catherine or her along, taking off into space. He'd bought a house, he said when he got back, by the sea. A home! A place to belong! She couldn't believe it! To leave No-Hope forever, to escape from the high school. To abandon the desolate neighborhood, where Jeanne-Louise, her only friend, had pulled up stakes and abandoned her! She'd clumped all over the flat in a victory dance, whooping and hollering until someone downstairs, The Creep probably, pounded in protest.

Because Vernon looked so tired, Shelley had bundled their furniture into a U-Haul, mostly by herself, not that there was all that much: The Joyners were not great on possessions. Vernon had disappeared with the U-Haul, for a second time alone, leaving Catherine and her to the untender mercies of her half-brother, Billy, and his wife. The third trip was now.

Shelley spotted an oil stove, obviously new, sitting on a shiny, metallic square of flooring, and she sighed in relief. Heat at least.

"Better light it," she ordered Vernon. "We're all cold." She looked past the living room into the cave of the kitchen, and her heart sank even lower, if possible. How *could* Catherine survive in this horrible place?

"I told you it needed fixing up," Vernon said unsteadily. "I'm going to do it. The kitchen things are coming tomorrow, but the stove's hooked up, Shelley, and the box. And there's water."

"God, what a dump! Vernon, you're really one damn fool." Catherine's whining grated on Shelley's ears. A little honest anger would have been more in order, but then Catherine's tantrums were no joy either. Half sympathetic, half downright annoyed, Shelley watched Catherine sink down at her familiar kitchen table.

And there she just sat. With her touched-up and coiffured blond hair, her light yellow pants suit, her bracelets, her earrings, her necklaces, the perfume, all the TV and magazine glitter. How could she possibly transplant to Sentinel Head? "You probably can't even *get* TV in this godforsaken place," Catherine said. Her face sagged into its habitual lines of discontent.

6

"TV was the first thing I asked about," Vernon said. "I'm not that much of a fool. There's a hair place in town, too." He clattered the oil burner, lit it, and slammed its door with unaccustomed anger.

"Would you two like some coffee?" Shelley asked. "If I can find the coffeepot?" Neither of them answered. She attacked a carton of kitchen things and snatched out the pot. "Well, *I'm* going to have some," she said with authority. "And so are you. Both of you."

Vernon slipped into the kitchen and stood behind one of the chairs. Shelley glanced back at him. Poor uncertain, apologetic Vernon, mousing along through life, asking only that he not create a disturbance. He was neither tall nor short, blond nor brunet, his face unremarkable. He'd held the same shipping-room job at the factory for years, probably because he wasn't aggressive enough to promote, but so conscientious that no one would consider replacing him. An unlikely husband for Catherine. Catherine, an unlikely wife for him.

"I was hoping that you two would like it here," Vernon said miserably. "That the two of you would find a life here together. That you could . . ." He seemed to collapse into a chair.

Shelley quietly set the coffeepot on the stove and then really turned in his direction. But he looks so frail! she thought with a shock. When had that happened? She hadn't noticed.

And this must be what retirement on disability meant. Vernon had always been sickly, given to spells. Why hadn't she figured it out sooner? In all the confusion of moving, was it that she hadn't had time, or perhaps occasion, to wonder? Or was it that she simply hadn't dared to ask?

Because now Vernon had answered her question before she'd ever asked it. "I was hoping the two of you would find a life here." That *you* could . . . Why hadn't he said *we?*

Because, if this *was* what the disability was about, Vernon was going to die, and she was going to be left here with Catherine! Alone, in this fog, this isolation. With each new thought Shelley felt colder. It was as if all the heat in her body had evaporated and she were turning to ice. Why had Vernon 'brought them here? Why did he intend to abandon them on Sentinel Head?

Shelley forced her hands to keep on working. She asked furious questions of herself, questions that had no answer. Why here? How long? Then what? Somehow she found three mugs and the spoons, the sugar bowl, the milk pitcher. She walked, like an automaton, back out to the car and collected the little sack of supper things she had bought in a town along the way. Mechanically, she fished out a carton of milk, a box of cookies.

Vernon and Catherine continued to sit without speaking at the table. If Catherine had grasped the import of Vernon's halting words, she gave no sign other than a low, despairing "bloody fool." Shelley managed a prick of pity for her. In fact, she felt suddenly sorry for both of them. Vernon, she noted, had withdrawn, as he often did, into himself, as if he had somehow made it here, to this place, and could not go one step farther. Shelley sighed.

She was used to Vernon's exhaustion and to Catherine's withdrawal into TV. Neither of her parents seemed able to cope, though Catherine was physically strong enough. They were only in their forties, yet Shelley thought of them as ancient, years older than the parents of any of her peers. Billy, her half-brother, Catherine's child, had been "difficult," as Vernon always said, and he'd mercifully pulled out at the first possible moment. That had left Shelley, at an early age, to take over completely.

She knew that people wondered about them. If Vernon and Catherine were an unlikely pair, she was even more an unlikely product of the two of them. She didn't even look like them, not like either of them. Jeanne-Louise had said Shelley looked like a figurehead on a ship, and she did. Yellow, flowing hair; painted blue eyes; a decided chin. Square and robust, she was designed to ride the ship through tempests at sea.

Going out to the car for the groceries, even in her state of shock, she'd heard the soughing of the ocean somewhere out there in the fog, a lonesome, still sound, but it wasn't anywhere near so lonesome or so still as this kitchen. She poured milk into the pitcher, and when she set it down on the table, it made a thump out of all proportion to such a simple gesture.

She was so alone! The Joyners never even related to each other, much less to anything outside. We really are zombies, she thought, three bodies floating around and past each other in strange rooms, hardly looking at one another, never ever touching. Here they were, surrounded by sea and fog, cut off from the human race entirely. Three lost souls. She looked over at Vernon in panic. How long would it be before there were only two?

She had to keep going. She ordered herself to pick up the milk carton, cross the floor, and open the refrigerator door.

In the sunny, lighted interior of the refrigerator, all by itself, sat a pie. A meringue hovered over it like a gigantic, fleecy cloud, and Shelley could see a line of its lemon filling underneath.

"Oh!" she gasped. *"Neighbors!"*

Vernon and Catherine came to life at the same moment and turned in her direction. They crowded, all three of them, around the refrigerator door. They must have looked like one of those Christmas paintings, an Adoration of the Magi, all three of them confounded by the light of that pie.

"It's the Brocks, I think," Vernon said huskily. "They're our closest neighbors."

Closest! Shelley was used to the shoulder jostling of factory homes. The Brocks, if they had brought the pie, were down the road, out of sight in the fog. But just the same someone, some *body*, was out there. Someone had lit up the black hole of that kitchen. *Somebody* was reaching out to them at the edge of desolation and pulling them back into the living world. Warmth returned to Shelley's body, as if someone had laid a thick wool shawl across her shoulders.

* * *

Later she knelt at her bedroom window upstairs. Her own room! For the first time in her whole life! She'd always bunked down wherever there was space—on a daybed, in the unused living room, as a rule. She'd never had any privacy, a place of her own. This room was stark enough: The wallpaper curled off and hung in strips from the slanted ceiling, and the steps upstairs had nearly catapulted her back to the first floor. But it didn't matter; it was *hers*. Warm air still drifted up from the oil stove through a grating in the floor, and she could hear the sea.

It was strange, but she felt at home now. It was the pie. It had broken through the isolation they'd all been feeling, and a sense of arrival had taken over— for her at least. She'd never lived anywhere near the sea, not in her whole life, but now she thought she had been here before or at least had somehow known about Sentinel Head, as if this was where she was meant to be.

She wanted suddenly to feel the outside; she needed to get even closer to this new place. She struggled with the window, dislodging flakes of old paint, but at last it gave way and shot upward with a bang. Nothing held the window up, and she propped it open with a wooden slat that lay on the sill, apparently put there for that purpose. She leaned out. The air smelled fresh, with almost a sting to it, and yet it was soft on her cheeks. A late seabird, flying past in the darkness, called its lonely cry.

Where was the bird going? Home to its nest in the rocks somewhere? A solitary bird, pulled through the fog and the night by some strong instinct for home, directed in its flight by some mysterious inner compass? Shelley listened until the bird's cry faded in the distance.

It *was* strange. Out of the debris of the day, to feel the rightness of this new place! If she'd had to hear Vernon's terrible, stumbling words at all, she was glad now that it was here, where she could sense that rightness. She wondered if the bird, alighting from its long, dark journey, felt a sense of homecoming like hers. It was something to think about, the power to fly home.

The slow rolling of the sea was making her sleepy, and she stood up. The fog sifted in through the window, softening the sharp edges of the funny iron bed Vernon had found for her. She felt impelled to make a statement, and for want of a better audience, she addressed the foggy window and whatever lay behind it.

"I'm going to stay," she said. "I'm going to *make* this place into a home. Even if I have to do it by myself. And no one's going to take it away from me either."

Chapter 2

SHELLEY HAD LONG SINCE LEARNED TO SLEEP through the factory whistle and far beyond, but next morning the sea gulls woke her at dawn. She dressed and edged her way down the tipsy stairs. It was still foggy, but when she opened the front door, a golden glow gave her hope that the fog might burn itself off. She looked into the dark living room and the darker kitchen beyond and longed to go and kick open the boarded-up front windows to let some light into the place. She flung the door wide open for light and was surprised to find the morning air so vigorous. She left the door open just the same.

Catherine's bedroom chopped off one end of the living room, and its door was firmly shut. It would be a long time before she stumbled out. Vernon, too, was apparently still asleep in his little room under the stair. No need to wake him up. Shelley tiptoed around the kitchen, gathering together what stores she had on hand, mostly bread for toast, and she ate as much breakfast as either of her parents would in a week. Each time she opened the fridge, she derived comfort and hope from the wonderful pie. No one had wanted to cut into it the night before—it would have been a sacrilege—but this morning she caved in and ate a large slab of it. After all, it would be mostly hers anyway; her parents would settle for only a small slice apiece.

This awful kitchen! And Catherine caged up in it day after day! She'd go crazy. Shelley, with regret, finished off the slice of pie, and looked hopelessly around. A lean-to, or little shed, had been tacked onto the house at the rear, next to Vernon's room, and it, too, opened into the kitchen. It was the bathroom. Catherine had sneered at its ancient fixtures, a tub on claws, for instance, that clutched the slanting floor, and a pump for the well that made a tattletale complaint every time anyone dared to use the water. Beside the pump, however, was a hot-water heater, like the oil stove, new. Shelley had been touched—although she couldn't help agreeing with Catherine about the fixtures—to see that Vernon had really been thinking of their comfort. When the thought that he was going to die knifed her, she resolutely pushed it back. She would have to live with that knowledge.

Part of the kitchen wall was covered with flimsy board strips, as if someone had hurriedly nailed a covering over windows or something. Shelley leaped to her feet. She tore at the boards with her bare hands and unveiled a perfectly good window.

"Shelley, if you're going to take that stuff down, find the hammer and use the claw!" Vernon said, walking rumpled from sleep into the kitchen. "There's a door there, too. I didn't have time to take all the boarding off." He tied his bathrobe around his waist, and Shelley saw with alarm how thin he was.

"How about the front windows?" Shelley asked, pushing back her anxiety. Vernon shook his head.

"They've never been finished," he said. "There's nothing there but a hole. But I'm going to do it," he promised, displaying a surprising vigor. In spite of his thinness, he really looked better than he had the night before—rested and somehow confident.

"Vernon, are you—" Shelley blurted out, but he firmly interrupted her.

"Not now, Shelley. Have you looked outside?" he asked with a smile, and Shelley, glancing toward the new window, got her first, sudden view of the distant sea to the south and west, the bay directly across from her.

The fog had lifted! She rushed to the front door, where the sun was already pushing into the room, and tried all in one gulp to take in the nearer eastern expanse of ocean in front of her, the far-off, curved beach and the opposite headland enclosing it, the cliffs and grassy headland to her right. Bursting out of doors, she turned to her left. Some way off, maybe as much as a city block, she could see a house.

"The ones who brought us the pie," Vernon said, stepping outside after her. "They're—" but he stopped as he saw her face and walked softly back inside. Shelley hardly saw him go. She only wanted to look, not talk, to take it all in. It wasn't so crazy at all, what Vernon had done. It was less and less a mistake—maybe no mistake at all!—that he had pulled out of No-Hope and brought them all here, to a little, unknown fishing village.

Shelley's further unveiling of the kitchen routed Catherine out of her bedroom. Shelley had expected the worst this morning, but for the moment Catherine looked almost happy. She always cheered up in the sunlight, and this morning sun was streaming in the front door, meeting the light from the newly revealed kitchen door and windows. Then she discovered her plants, which Vernon had trucked up with the furniture, alive and well, sitting outside. Somebody had been watering them for her all week while Vernon closed out the odds and ends of his life in No-Hope. She was really pleased. Shelley gave a sigh of relief. Obviously, if these small acts of friendship—the pie and the watering of the plants—had occurred, Vernon must have broken through his habitual reserve and talked to people. It was a good omen.

Just the same, Shelley wanted to get on with her life, and the two of them were underfoot.

"We need groceries," she pointed out. "Yesterday I only got things for last night, and I have a list."

"There aren't any stores out here on the Head," Vernon explained. "You have to drive into Port Huyett. That's the nearest town." He pointed in the general direction of the curved beach that Shelley had spotted out the front door. "We're going to have to learn we can't just run down to a corner grocery. Sentinel Head is really only a neighborhood, sort of a suburb of Port Huyett. There aren't more than thirty or forty families out here, all told."

"Then how am I going to get into town—if there's anything there in the first place?" Catherine stopped midway across the kitchen, plant in hand. "I don't intend to sit around waiting for you to take me," she added harshly. Shelley held her breath: It had all gone so well so far.

"The Halifax bus stops on the trunk road twice a day," Vernon answered shortly. "Most people just stand at the crossroads until somebody comes along and gives them a lift." Vernon turned aside, as if to avoid having to answer more.

"Vernon, why don't you take Catherine to town right now? So she can see it," Shelley suggested. Or rather ordered, and they both began to get ready. Shelley glanced at them once or twice, checking automatically, as if they were children needing to catch the school bus. Sometimes she felt as if she'd been *born* in charge! It had always been Vernon and Catherine, never Mother and Dad, as with other people's parents.

"They'll be bringing a kitchen cabinet," Vernon explained, standing in the doorway. "Show them where it goes. They're bringing a desk for you, too," he added. "The things aren't new, but I got extra money for retirement. Enough to fix things up a little."

Shelley's excitement about the unfolding day reflected back to him, and a shy smile came over his face. But it vanished immediately, as if he had begun to hope for one minute but then didn't quite dare to after all or at least not for too long at a time.

"Be sure they take the desk upstairs. I can't do heavy work like that anymore," he said quietly. Shelley nodded, feeling the stab again.

Finally the Ford took off, jolting its way back to the asphalt, and Shelley was alone in the house. She drew a long breath. She would start with the cartons.

But there was something she had to do first, a ritual that she had to attend to. Life broke itself up into phases, and she had to do away with one phase before she started the next. She walked to the door, and glanced up and down the road to make sure that no one was advancing from either direction. Then she crossed to the other side and walked down through a patch of foot-tangling undergrowth to the rocks that lined the sea below. She scrambled over the boulders, planning to get very close to the water;

but the rocks at the water's edge turned out to be wet and slippery.

Shelley looked around for a flat rock that she could stand on and, finding one, gathered up a handful of smaller stones. She arranged them on a rock above her, in order of size, starting with the largest. Then carefully balancing, and after one more hurried look to make sure that she was indeed alone, she turned and faced the water.

"All *right!*" she yelled into the wind. "This is the end! *No-Hope*"—she picked up the largest rock—"INTO THE SEA!" At the splash, an Apache war whoop and dance on the flat rock.

"MACKENZIE HIGH SCHOOL! INTO THE SEA!" Splash, war whoop, stamping.

"JOHN LAIDLAW, PRINCIPAL! INTO THE SEA!" Third splash, war whoop, and dance.

"ALEXANDER BICKMAN, GEOMETRY TEACHER! INTO THE SEA!" Frenzied war whoop and dance.

Shelley was just starting on JOHN EDWARD HOPPER, CREEP IN THE APARTMENT DOWNSTAIRS, when she heard a laugh. Her heart sinking, she looked up and saw a boy, about her own age or a little older, standing on the rock edge above her. From the horrible look of things, he had been standing there for quite a while. He was holding a large fish by the eye sockets and swinging it gently back and forth. He wore dark green work clothes and rubber boots. His black hair curled about his round face and a pronounced cleft in his chin gave him a puckish look that matched the merriment in his eyes. Shelley knew at once that he was by far the cutest boy she had ever seen in her whole entire life. She also saw that he was laughing heartily. At her.

"Who's next?" he asked with interest.

"The Creep Downstairs," said Shelley in desperation. There was no logical retreat other than hurling herself after the stones, so she might as well charge straight ahead. "Where I came from. John Edward Hopper."

The fish bringer was still waiting and laughing. "You've got two more stones," he pointed out.

"Next my half-brother, Billy, and his nitwit wife." Shelley hesitated. "And then Jeanne-Louise."

"Who's Jeanne-Louise?" he asked. He was really interested.

"I *thought* she was my friend. But when she moved, she never even wrote a postcard."

"I'm not much of a hand at writing, either," he observed. He swung the fish. "If she was a good friend once, maybe that's all you need."

"Right," Shelley said, dropping the last rock back onto the shore but tossing the others out to sea one after the other. "I didn't want to pitch her off like that anyway. She was really a good friend. I'm Shelley Joyner," she said matter-of-factly. "Newly arrived."

"Arlan Brock," he answered formally, though his eyes continued to laugh at her. His shirt was open at the neck, and his muscular arms had not gotten that way from shoving weights around in the school gym. He looked a lot more like a man than a high-school boy. "I've brought you a fish," he said.

"Do I have to carry it by the eyes?" Shelley scrambled up the rocks. Arlan was tall, and he looked down at her.

"I'll carry it for you," he said gravely.

"Arlan, I haven't any idea what you do with such a big fish. Did your mother make that elegant pie? Would she tell me how to cook a fish? Do you leave the skin on?"

"Skin?" Arlan looked puzzled, as if things had begun to whirl around in front of him.

"Well, scales, then."

"I'll clean it for you, Shelley," he said, again gravely.

"You can show me how, and then I can do it."

He had left a pan and a knife on the rock edge. He laid the fish out on a rock. "Haddie," he said.

"That knife looks really lethal."

"We call them rippers," Arlan explained.

"Jack the Ripper."

Arlan laughed and looked at his knife as if he'd never seen one like it before in his life. "I mean to remember that name. I like it." He deftly cleaned the fish.

"Wow," said Shelley.

"It's nice you've come, Shelley," Arlan said. They walked back to the house together, leaving the gulls to fight over the fish remains.

"Come down for tea when you can," Arlan said. "Mum will tell you how to cook haddie." He gave her the pan and smiled down at her, and it wasn't just a short, well-good-bye-now smile, either.

Shelley watched him stride down the road toward his house. Then she drew a long breath and went inside. It was up to her to make a home out of chaos. She'd promised herself that. She walked to the front door again and looked out over the sunny water. The breeze played about in her hair. The last of the gulls, disappointed in their share of the haddie, straggled complaining out to sea. The air was sweet with a grassy fragrance, and fresh in a way she had never imagined. Arlan, small in the distance, disappeared. Shelley smiled, to no one in particular, to everything in general.

Chapter 3

TWO MEN ARRIVED IN A PICKUP AND BROUGHT IN the cabinet and desk that Vernon had bought. The cabinet was really an old-fashioned kitchen sideboard, put together, probably, by a fisherman during the winter months when he wasn't mending nets. It had been well used, by a family, Shelley assumed, and she liked that. A whole succession of kids must have done their homework on the desk and then grown up and gone away, abandoning it.

The men took the desk upstairs and asked if they could help her with anything else. She had them move the china cupboard from the living room into the end of the kitchen that she was fixing up for Catherine. It left the living room bare, except for the daybed and a couple of chairs, but who was going to sit in there anyway, with the windows all boarded up? She stole the living-room rug and put that on the kitchen floor to cover up the deplorable, overlapping sheets of old linoleum.

It was crazy, she supposed, but much later, when she surveyed her work, she realized that her refrain all morning had been "Will Catherine like this? Would Catherine like that?" It was important. Catherine *had* to like it. She'd tried to fix up a pretty place for Catherine. She'd hung curtains from the old apartment and dug out the familiar table cover. And in the end, the kitchen had turned out to be halfway cozy. Shelley looked it over with satisfaction but with some doubt, too. Catherine might not be all that caring.

As a final touch, Shelley rolled the TV from the living room and hooked it up. She thought briefly of smashing its smug face but instead she put it carefully in the dark corner, where Catherine could watch it without looking into the light.

It took Shelley two minutes by the clock to arrange the living room, and it looked hideous.

Another truck pulled up in front of the house, and Arlan and his father got out. They had brought a rocking chair and a cupboard to put over the sink.

"Been out in the shed," Arlan's father said. "Not much use out there." He looked around the kitchen. "Not too bad," he commented. "Always been a good sturdy house. Reedie never got to finish her out." He was as fair as Arlan was dark, ruddy faced from fishing and as powerfully built as Arlan was going to be someday. Shelley was to call him Axel. Axel and

Arlan had brought tools with them, and in a few minutes they easily had the cupboard on the wall.

"The rocking chair belongs in the kitchen," Arlan said. "Got to have a rocker for the Old One to fall into when he gets home from sea." He nudged his father with his elbow, and Axel made a laughing pass back at him. The gesture, the easy joshing, filled Shelley with longing, and she hastily turned away.

"Mum's waiting tea," Arlan said and smiled at her. For a moment Shelley hesitated, not sure what the custom was. Tea at this hour? Arlan's face showed a trace of worry.

"You have to," he said with sincerity. "It's neighborly. And we drink tea all day long around here."

Shelley laughed. "We'll try to be neighborly, Arlan," she promised. "Even if we're not very good at it. And I'd love some tea."

"Out here we have to depend on each other," Axel said soberly. He held the door open for her. "It's all we have sometimes."

Axel crawled into the truck; and in a moment Shelley was tucked in between the two of them, and they drove back to the Brocks'.

There was something self-assured about the way the Brocks' house heeled into the rocky soil, as if it had weathered a lot of storms and intended to weather a lot more. It had been a relief to discover that the old Reedie place was sturdy, but Shelley couldn't help envying the soft yellow of the Brocks' newly painted shingles, the blue shutters, and the rounded bay window in front, crisscrossed with priscillas.

Inside, not only was Arlan's house spotless, but everything gleamed with varnish, like pictures of a yacht. The huge kitchen and more formal sitting room were filled with handcraft: carved and beautifully varnished wooden plaques of fishing boats and homemade whatnots filled with flowered teacups.

"Arlan," commented Axel. "Handy with tools."

There were crocheted pillows on the sofa, doilies on the chairs, on the wall was an embroidered picture of fishermen at sea. In the kitchen there were tea towels, owl pot holders, and even little booties for the legs of the table.

"Mum," said Arlan solemnly. "Handy with the needle."

Shelley liked Arlan's mother, Dru, right away, probably because she looked so much like Arlan, or he like her. She was small and compact, a lot faster on her feet than either Arlan or his father. Bumping into them in her bustle, she set the towering men to one side like chessmen. She laughed a lot—perhaps you would call her merry, except that in repose her face showed a lot more than laughter. Shelley thought about Catherine's longing for glamour: Dru wouldn't know what she was even talking about. Presently Clyde, Arlan's older brother, came in from outside to meet her, and Shelley and Dru were surrounded by giants. Clyde was blond and ruddy like his father and even bigger. He was married to a girl named Gail and lived several houses away, but he fished with Axel and obviously took orders from him as well, at least at sea. Axel, in fact, ran the family like the skipper of a boat.

When the Brock family sat down around the table for tea, they drew Shelley into the circle with them, as naturally as if they'd been neighbors forever.

Shelley wanted to cartwheel home, and she would have, too, if it hadn't been both undignified and physically impossible. The ingathering of the Brock family had been so right, what she had always missed. During the one hour she had spent with the Brocks, she could actually feel the city loneliness of years drop away. Her feeling the night before had been right. But how had she known?

They'd teased her about the haddie, a girl not knowing how to cook a fish.

"Doesn't your mother cook?" Dru had asked in surprise.

"I'm chief cook and bottle washer," she'd answered to her own surprise without embarrassment. She'd caught the questioning look that passed between Dru and Axel, and that hadn't bothered her either.

"Your father's not well, is he?" Axel had asked.

"No, he's not," she'd answered, wishing it weren't so obvious. Why had she missed it before now?

Axel, looking grave, had said, "You must call on us if you need us, Shelley."

School, it turned out, was to start in about a week. Arlan had one more term to go; he was making up one term when he'd dropped out to fish. Then he was going to try for the Coast Guard.

"After the spring lobstering," Clyde had warned.

"Yes," Arlan had agreed. They all had a funny way of saying *yes*, as if they were gasping for air at the same time they said it. Right there in the middle of the road where no one could hear her, Shelley tried it, but it didn't work.

"It's hard to go to a new school the first day. I'll pick you up and walk you down to the bus stop, Shelley, and introduce you around." Arlan had said that just as she left.

It gave the final lift to the day.

Shelley spotted the Ford in front of her house. Her folks were home. She bounded in the front door.

"Well, where have *you* been?" Catherine asked before Shelley could draw her breath. She looked at Catherine in bewilderment, at her petulant face. Why was she so upset all of a sudden?

"I've been at the Brocks'. Our next-door neighbors," Shelley answered. "Arlan brought us a fish."

"And just who is this Arlan?" Catherine asked with suspicion, and Shelley felt the glow she'd brought back with her begin to fade away.

"He's the boy next door," Shelley said. "He's really nice."

"Just one minute," Catherine said. "I'm not sure I want you batting around with these people. We don't know them. This is just a little fishing village!"

"What's the matter with fishermen?" Shelley demanded. "Their house is a lot nicer than ours will ever be. Arlan's really neat. He's going to call for me the first day of school and introduce me to the other kids."

"Now, look here, Shelley," Catherine said, "I don't want you taking up with the first boy that comes along."

Shelley glared at her. Having Catherine suddenly come to life and begin to order her around was the last thing she'd asked for. Her whole attitude was ridiculous anyhow. *Arlan* was the one who had every right to be talking down his neighbors.

"If I want to go out with fishermen, I'll go out with fishermen," Shelley said steadily. "With Arlan or anyone else."

"For once," Catherine shouted, "you listen to your mother! Your father may have brought us to this godforsaken place, but that doesn't mean . . ."

The bedroom door opened, and Vernon walked into the kitchen.

"Be quiet, Catherine," he said. He looked white and drawn, and his face was tight with pain. "Shelley's grandfather was a fisherman, as you well know. He was a fine man, and I should have had sense enough to follow in his footsteps."

"I suppose you think I was the one who ruined your life," Catherine snapped at him.

"I didn't say that, Catherine," Vernon replied.

Shelley groaned. "Oh, come on, you two," she said, but they paid no attention to her.

"Well, I don't see why you've brought us to this stinking part of the world anyhow. Not that New Hope was any Eden," Catherine yelled. "Don't think I wouldn't have left a long time ago if I'd had any choice."

Shelley winced. "Why did you bring us here, Vernon?" she asked peaceably. "How did you find this place?" But she broke off abruptly. Pain seemed suddenly to claw at Vernon, and he bent over.

"Water, Shelley . . ." She helped him into the rocker and hastily filled a glass at the sink. He closed his eyes for a while.

"I took a long chance, Shelley," he said at last. "I hoped you'd take to this place. You too, Catherine," he added quietly.

Shelley laid her hand on Vernon's shoulder. "It's going to work, Vernon," she said.

"Not for me, it isn't," Catherine retorted, still furious. "I'm getting out the first minute I can."

"Don't start that all over again, Catherine," Vernon said wearily. "I've told you a hundred times you could go. But if you're going to stay, you're to leave Shelley alone."

Catherine directed a look of sheer hatred at Vernon—or was it just the ultimate in frustration? Where could Catherine go? Shelley thought, momentarily sorry for her. With a shrug, her usual answer to the unanswerable, Catherine turned on the TV and sat down at the table, her back to Shelley and Vernon. The familiar prattle filled the kitchen, and the waving arms and gesticulations of the TV people took over the corner of Shelley's eye.

"I didn't know my grandfather was a fisherman. I thought he worked in the Sidney mines," Shelley said softly, glancing at Catherine. She had probably not floated off with the story, appearances to the contrary. No point in getting her all stirred up again.

"No," said Vernon. "Your grandfather worked in the mines after the war, but he was always a fisherman at heart. He was torpedoed during the war, you know, and he was never right after that. He died when I was a little boy. He met your grandmother when he was in the service, and they lived in several places; he tried several kinds of jobs. They even did some farming, out in Manitoba. But they ended up in Sidney. He hated the mines, but sometimes you get caught in life, Shelley. He was really a fisherman," Vernon insisted, as if this were the most important thing in the world. Shelley wondered, in some panic, if he were going to cry; he seemed so upset. "Your grandfather was meant to live by the water," he repeated tearfully.

"Are you all right, Vernon?" Shelley asked anxiously. He nodded, but he looked lost in the Brocks' enormous rocker.

"Listen to me, Shelley," Vernon said desperately. "You have to go your own way. You're going to have to work things out yourself. You're going to have to make your own home." He jerked his head toward Catherine. "*She* can't help you," he said bitterly. "She's more apt to get in your way. And there's a limit to what you can do to help her. Don't forget that." He closed his eyes again.

No point in asking him, no need to ask him, what all this meant. It was as plain as the nose on her face. She was going to lose Vernon. And what if Catherine decided to move back to her old haunts in No-Hope, dragging Shelley with her? Catherine could, Shelley knew. She was still a minor and would be for two more years.

"What if—?" she started to ask Vernon, but he looked too sick, too spent. She couldn't harry him with questions like that. She would have to deal with Catherine—alone.

And that wasn't going to be easy. Shelley realized with amazement that in one day she had come to think of Sentinel Head as home, as a place where she wanted to stay. And her biggest job would be keeping Catherine happy and contented, so that *she* would stay.

Vernon was dying. You couldn't get around that. Shelley felt a wave of weariness, of loneliness so deep that she wanted to cry out. She leaned against the stove: How *was* she to cope? But then she straightened. The Brock family was down the road, and in two days Arlan would pick her up and take her away, if only to the bus stop.

Chapter 4

IT WAS JUST BARELY SEPTEMBER, AND ON THE FIRST day of school Arlan called for Shelley. Catherine wasn't up yet, but to avoid any possible encounter with her, Shelley waited for Arlan outside the front door. When he walked up the road, she thought he looked as much at home in jeans and T-shirt as he did in his fisherman's work clothes and just as nice. Arlan had a wonderful way of making someone feel wanted, as if he were really interested. Shelley thought he had probably had hundreds of girlfriends if he was as easy with them as he was with her.

They walked the considerable distance out to the trunk road, chatting and laughing, to where the school bus would pick them up. In and out of the conversation, Shelley wondered how Arlan would manage this new girl on the block—would he sit with her on the bus, for instance? As it turned out, when they reached the little group waiting there, he introduced her to Janet Crawford and strolled off casually to wait with the other guys. He'd worked it out beforehand, Shelley guessed. He'd probably figured she'd like Janet, because there were other girls standing around that he might have introduced.

Janet would be the first one you noticed in a group, particularly if you were a stranger meeting everyone for the first time. She didn't wait to see what kind of person you turned out to be. Her face lit up just because you were there, and this made her eyes even bigger and more violet than they already were. Shelley envied Janet's short, wavy hair, which the damp sea wind lifted and rearranged around her face, as if it were trying out various new styles.

While they waited for the bus, Janet kept up a running line of funny stories. Everyone liked her; that was obvious. She was going with a guy from Port Huyett, which maybe gave her a special status, but

31

that wasn't all. She was just a nice person. She took Shelley under her wing, inviting her to share a seat when the bus came.

"That Arlan!" she confided under cover of the bus racket. "He's a loner. Oh, my dear, what a waste! He's *never* going to ask a girl out, I don't think."

"Oh?" asked Shelley, surprised.

Janet glanced at Shelley. "He's biding his time," she explained. "Arlan's got everything charted out, near fifty years ahead. He's set on going into the Coast Guard. He's the same way about girls. When he decides, he'll stick with it, I bet, through hell and high water."

"Oh," said Shelley again. She'd been wrong about Arlan and girls, and she was sorry about it. Maybe she'd have had some chance with him if she was just one of many, though even that wasn't sure. Jeanne-Louise, her lost friend from No-Hope, had known instinctively what to do about boys. Shelley, in the background, had watched her operate but had never really learned how she did it. Shelley sighed and turned toward the window, anxious to see what the area looked like.

The sea was everywhere, in bays and inlets, tidal backwaters and salt marshes, around every curve. Bordering the various neighborhoods that the school bus passed through lay the forest—miles, she knew, of muskeg, swamp, and hillock. The Joyners had cut through this forest on their way across the island, and then they had followed it to Sentinel Head. It had added to their sense of isolation that day.

The homes that the bus passed were modest, some as nice as the Brocks' or bigger, some even more hopeless and down at the heels than the Joyners'.

The bus crossed a causeway, a thin road with a salt marsh on one side and only a frail rim of sand dune on the other, holding back what seemed to be an awful lot of ocean. The high school was at the end of the causeway and looked out over the huge, curved beach that Shelley could see from her front door at home. From here, Sentinel Head, which she could just glimpse, was as bleak as a moonscape.

The bus pulled up to the school door.

"I was wishing it would take us through Port Huyett," Shelley told Janet. "My father was really done in after all the effort of getting here, and we just sat around all weekend. Not that that was so horrible," she added hastily. "There's an awful lot a landlubber like me can learn just staying home." Janet laughed. "Just the same," Shelley added. "I still haven't seen Port Huyett."

"I don't know that you've missed too much," Janet observed. "But we can just stay on if you like. The bus picks up some kids on the other side of the town and comes right back." They sat back down.

"Tour bus," Janet explained to the other kids.

The bus circled Port Huyett, picking up kids from its outer limits. Some of the homes in town were old and past their prime, but they had an air of distinction, as if times had been easier once—for some people at least. A narrow street of unbeautiful storefronts and snack places led to the harbour, where two fish plants stood, separated by a restaurant. The latter was called the Harbour Gull, and Shelley thought it was well named, for gulls swooped all over the place. The harbour was not all picturesque, and some of it was pretty grubby, a collection of salt-scoured wooden buildings. The plant workers in their white aprons, gathering for the day's work, evinced no joy that Shelley could see.

They rumbled past the second fish plant. "It looks like a prison," Shelley commented.

"Both fish plants are," Janet responded soberly. "But they're about the only places to work around here. For women anyway. Mother works at the Gull. She knows."

They passed a beverage room, a not unattractive tavern jutting out over the water. *The Dragger.*

"Sort of a sad place," Janet pointed out. "People hang out there, sit around most of the day. I guess they haven't anything else to do."

The Dragger. There was one in about every town, it seemed like. Places where people sat and whiled away endless time. At one of these places in No-Hope, Catherine had found a friend, a sometime bar girl and waitress. Every day Catherine had wandered down to Pete's Place, sitting at her own little table, drinking coffee, joined by Mary Ann in between her not too pressing chores. Between them, they'd fabricated the life they ached to live, away from the ugliness of the factory town, in a kept leisure somewhere, a world of luxury unattainable by either of them.

Not that Catherine hadn't tried to break loose from her disappointing life. Shelley remembered violent fights between her parents—Catherine demanding money, for clothes usually, Vernon doggedly fighting back or ignoring her complaints altogether. He didn't bother to look at the pictures of cruises to the Caribbean she pressed on him; he didn't even glance into the windows of the fancy restaurants they passed on their rare visits to St. John or Fredericton. When Mary Ann was snatched away by her husband to Toronto, Catherine was despondent. Exasperated, Vernon finally suggested she try to find some work for herself, to help out, but she reacted so violently, and with such scorn over his inability to support her, that he never tried again. For the last couple of years, Catherine had lived in self-imposed apathy, relieved only by TV.

Port Huyett wasn't going to offer much to Catherine, Shelley concluded; that was clear. Except for the Dragger.

A bunch of kids were waiting for them when they got back to the high school, others joined them, and they all walked in together. When they heard that Shelley came from the house above Arlan's out on the Head, they whistled. "You the new folks in the Reedie place?" Shelley liked the kids—most of them. They were open and friendly, and the halls echoed with strong Nova Scotian voices.

The teachers looked like teachers anywhere, but the principal was a shock. To begin with, she was a woman, and Shelley hadn't expected it. Sarah Luddington barely reached to the shoulders of many of her students: Most of girls looked heartier, more robust, somehow, than she. She seemed to come from another world, a far-off place of business executives, lawyers, and people in big cities. Her trim suit and shiny pumps were at complete odds with the casual dress of both faculty and students, along with her rather aristocratic air and her deep, correct voice. Shelley couldn't see her running the school, not these grown-up kids, most of whom already knew what earning a living from the sea was all about. Janet shook her head.

"She's one tough lady," she said with feeling. "Oh, my dear!"

The kids walked on the beach at lunchtime. The others were used to beaches, but Shelley wanted to turn somersaults. Instead she danced up and down on the hard sand. The girls all laughed.

"Wait till the winter storms," they chanted, and in tune with the waves, they sang the little chorus Shelley had first smiled at but already had begun to like. "Oh, my dear, oh, my dear!"

On the noisy bus ride home, Shelley sat again with Janet.

"Hey, Janet!" one of the girls called to her over the banter and laughter. "You and Craig going to the Center tonight?"

"Nope," Janet replied. "Craig's out to sea."

"Hey, Shelley," the girl then said, "We're walking out tonight, meet at the crossroads. Want to come?" Shelley, not quite understanding, glanced at Janet. Janet shook her head.

"It's OK if you know what you're getting into. You don't know the people around here yet," she said in a low voice.

"Guess not," Shelley called back. "We're still unpacking. Thanks, though."

"It's not hard to get picked up by the wrong guys," Janet explained softly. "The ones you want to know—well, they don't drive around like that very much. It's hard to get to know them sometimes. The families are sort of close around here, see."

Shelley glanced quickly at Janet—was it a warning, she wondered, not to get too pushy? But Janet smiled at her.

"You get kind of tired of the same old gang. Mum says over the years there's been too much intermarriage. Everyone seems to be related, somewhere back. *I'm* glad you've come from outside, but sometimes people think it's hard to break in."

It was a warning, then, but a nice one. If Janet liked her, maybe it would be easier. Or if Arlan liked her. Maybe she'd fit in after a while. She wondered about Vernon, so frail, among these strong fishing folk. Catherine would never be part of them, ever.

After the bus had let the kids off and they had filtered off into their various homes, Shelley and Arlan ended up walking up the road alone.

"It's going to be a lovely evening," he said with a funny smile.

"The girls are going to walk out after supper," Shelley told him. "They're meeting at the crossroads."

Arlan gave her a quick, searching look.

"I'm not sure what this walking out means," she explained. "They didn't do it where I came from. At

37

least I don't think so. Anyhow Janet said not to go unless I knew people better."

"Why don't you walk out with me, Shelley?" he asked and grinned down at her. "You know me."

"Could we go out on the Head?" Shelley asked. "I'm dying to see what's out there."

Arlan's eyes twinkled. "If the kids on the bus hear about it, they'll think I'm some fast worker."

"Oh!" said Shelley, understanding suddenly. She felt her face growing hot. "I didn't mean . . ."

Arlan took her hands in his and looked down at her. Laughter lingered around his mouth and eyes, but his voice was serious. "Shelley," he said, "no one tells me what to do, and not many tell you, I don't think. I'll pick you up right after supper. Bring a jacket."

Shelley wasn't much of a reader, still less a TV watcher, but she'd known in her bones there was someplace in the world like this headland. After a short walk seaward up the road, she and Arlan came to Jaimie's sheep gate. It was chained shut, and Arlan helped her over the fence. As she landed with finality on the other side, she remembered Jeanne-Louise. She'd have floated over and landed on one toe like a ballet dancer. Still, Arlan in his heavy boots didn't look as if he'd have been all that impressed with Jeanne-Louise, and the thought gave Shelley some comfort.

"You're going to get your sneakers wet, Shelley," Arlan said as they started up the rough path.

"The dew's fallen already. You need some hiking boots for the rocks around here."

"Hiking boots are a *long* way down the list, Arlan." Shelley laughed. It was really funny. Hiking boots were absolutely out of sight. Arlan gave her another of his quick looks.

"The path along the sea edge is easier. The sheep tamp it down," he said. As Arlan steered her up a byway, she saw that the moor was crisscrossed with sheep paths. She didn't see any sheep.

"Probably back in the barn," Arlan explained. "Jaimie uses the old farmhouse as a sheep barn."

They topped a little rise, reaching the ocean edge, and Shelley came to a sudden halt, too overwhelmed to speak. A winding path led upward to the point ahead of her. Below, the swells broke with a throaty sound on the huge rocks. From here she could really see the whole sweep of ocean, the view she had seen only partially from the kitchen window. The sun was low in the sky, and the water, not yet picking up the sunset colors, was a succession of dark and darker blues all the way to the horizon.

"Is that *west?*" Shelley asked, puzzled. "The sunset? Here on this coast?"

Arlan laughed. "You're on a finger of land, don't forget. It has two sides. Anyway, Nova Scotia doesn't lie north and south of its length. You tell people the sun sets outside your window into the bay, and they think you're nuts."

In the other direction, as they looked across Sentinel Head and the intervening water, the opposite and enclosing headland was a long way off.

From here, Shelley could see only a piece of the crescent beach where she had danced at lunchtime. On the moor, sitting exposed to the weather and in stark isolation, was Jaimie's barn, a low, ground-hugging farmhouse. Shingled and long unpainted, it melded into the rock colors and the soft gray-green of the turf. From its upstairs dormer windows, surely there must be one of the loveliest views in the world.

Arlan and Shelley walked out to the end of Sentinel Head, climbing higher as they approached the tip. At one point, the path came close to the sea edge, and Shelley, looking down its precipitous slope, shivered.

"It would be awful if a sheep fell down there," she said. Arlan nodded.

"They do, though, sometimes. Jaimie keeps a watch. But he's getting old, and it's hard for him to get way out here. He worries about it." The grass ended, and they entered the realm of the birds.

"Willet," Arlan said as a sharp-billed, brown-and-white bird scolded at them. "Go on, get lost. We're not after your nest."

They had to rock climb to the tip. Combers rolled in from the sea, broke on shoals some distance out, and thundered into the rocks far below them. The incoming sea awed and frightened Shelley, and as the wind tore at her, she unashamedly held onto Arlan.

"Some dangerous shoals," Arlan commented. "Have to steer far clear of them."

Shelley wanted to see Jaimie's barn from closer

up, so they returned by a perilous—and what Arlan explained was a little-used—path between the crags that made up the head. They crossed a small cove, where the waves, coming in, rolled back a beachful of small, round stones and then released them. The stones grumbled all the way back to the sea. It was a wild and lonely area, Sentinel Head. Shelley loved it, and she wished she were part of it, not an outsider but someone that this place, by long use, belonged to, like Arlan. He was comfortable here, he and his family, in a way she had no right to be but somehow, surprisingly, was.

As they neared the farmhouse, Arlan spotted Jaimie's truck. "He'll probably tear into us," he said. "He'll jump to all the wrong conclusions."

"I thought you didn't let people tell you what to do."

"Jaimie Wenloch's something else," Arlan said.

Jaimie, crowded by his sheep, was sorting sacks of feed. One arm hung useless by his side, but with the other he dragged and yanked the heavy bags.

"Hurt in the war," Arlan said in an undertone. "Had to give up fishing."

Jaimie looked up, glancing first at Arlan. He nodded in recognition, if not cordiality, and then he turned to Shelley. An extraordinary change came over his weather-beaten, bitter face. There was a second of apparent shock, and then the old man flew into a rage.

"What are you doing out here with that girl, Arlan Brock?" he roared. "You lay hands on her, you do wrong by her out here like the others, and I'll

41

have you by the shanks of your legs. Now get her back home." He stood there in the midst of the milling sheep, trembling with rage and shaking his fist at Arlan.

"We were just out walking, Mr. Wenloch," Shelley said, determined to stand her ground. "That's all." He glared at her, then turning back to Arlan and, still agitated, shouted, "You don't bring her out here to this place. You hear me?"

Arlan and Shelley walked back to the gate. "That's some strange," Arlan said thoughtfully. "He seems to think he knows you."

Shelley shook her head. "How could he possibly?" she asked.

Old Jaimie

Jaimie, trembling and shaken, watched Arlan and the girl walk toward the gate. He hadn't expected this at all. He'd written off his concern about the Joyners in the Reedie place. He'd seen the man as he drove past, a sickly looking fellow, not long for this world, he thought, and bearing no resemblance whatever to the Conrad Joyner he had known. Some other family, a coincidence of names, he'd concluded, and put it out of mind. But just now Conrad Joyner in the form of Arlan's girl had stood before him. Conrad Joyner's blue eyes had bored into him.

It had been a shock. He'd taken the only possible course open to him and chewed Arlan out.

Jaimie finished his chores, climbed painfully into the truck, and drove home. He lived in town, in Port Huyett, where he'd found Maiz and married her. He himself had grown up on Sentinel Head, and even after these long years, the Head, rather than Port Huyett, was home to him. His father and grandfather before him had owned the land where he grazed his sheep; and his grandparents, the old ones, had actually lived in the farmhouse.

He'd been a fisherman in his youth, though the war had finished that off, and he still loved and respected the sea and needed to live near it. He had compromised with Maiz, who hadn't wanted to leave the town, not even for Sentinel Head, and they had built a small house in Port Huyett as close to the water's edge as safety allowed.

Once home, he reached in his cupboard and fished out a bottle of rum. He kept it there against emergency or unexpected company, but not having had either one recently, it had hardly seen the light of day. Jaimie put the bottle in front of him on the table and sat down painfully in an old captain's chair, one that offered his body some support. He was lonely: Two years had not one whit diminished his loneliness for Maiz, and this sudden evocation of his past was almost more than he could bear.

Martin Brock, Conrad Joyner, and Jaimie himself. Three lads, though he was the oldest of the three, and they'd grown up together. They'd signed on the same draggers, they'd lobstered together, they'd got up a sum and bought their own trawler. When the war came to England, they'd signed on the same ship, running supplies to the mother country through the North Sea route.

Conrad had been a slow, easy, blond chap, big fellow with blue eyes that could bore holes in you. He eventually married a girl in the service and went off with her. What had happened to him? Or had he heard once that Conrad had died? Jaimie shook his head.

When they were torpedoed, Martin Brock had gone down at once. Never even got to see Axel, his baby son. Jaimie himself was shot to hell. When he got back, after months in a hospital, Conrad had disappeared, gone from his life forever.

Jamie, and Maiz with him, had been good to Martin's widow and the young Axel. Axel had turned out well, and Arlan, coming along, wasn't the worst of the young, though what he was doing out on the Head he didn't like to think. The cliffs were full of hidey-holes, and Jaimie knew full well what went on inside them. Damn kids. When he was their age, he'd worked. He hadn't had time to lollygag all over town.

Jaimie stared at the bottle in front of him. He'd have to find out about these Joyners. Had Conrad had a son? A granddaughter? If so, why had they come here? Jaimie opened the bottle and poured out a good four fingers. The agony of its drinking did him good. Then he got to his feet, stowed the bottle in the recesses of the cupboard, and went to bed.

Chapter 5

NO ONE EXPECTED SEPTEMBER TO BE SO LOVELY. The days were mostly fine. Shelley started out each day by falling a little more in love with Sentinel Head. Sometimes she'd climb out on the rocks and just sit and look at the ocean. It was as if she had to absorb all its beauty at once to make up for lost time, for the wasted years when she'd been somewhere else. She'd never seen such blue before, never expected the vibrancy of sea and sky. Or real sunshine. It was a warm color, like fire, and bore no relationship whatever to the insipid lemon that sifted down around the factory and the houses huddled along the No-Hope streets.

Sometimes a light sea fog dimmed their going to school, but it burned off by midmorning. They had some rain at night, but no real storms. Some of the roadside flowers began to fade and dry up, but Shelley couldn't get used to the extravagance of the free bouquets that were left. The kids laughed at her as she gathered armfuls and took them home.

Things were going better there than she had hoped. After the fight over Arlan and Catherine's bitter words to Vernon, Shelley noted a change between the two of them, a sort of companionship. Vernon was the engineer of it, and Shelley thought it was rather touching. Perhaps he was hoping to re-create what had been lost over the years, or maybe he was trying to help Catherine adjust to this new life. Shelley could only hope it would work.

Sunday morning, with light winds, the radio said, and a calm sea stirred only by a succession of swells that broke up into a lacy frill at the shore. Shelley walked down to the water's edge in front of the house and sat on a rock, wondering all over again why anyone would want to be anywhere but there. She dreamily watched the gulls circle and suddenly swoop seaward. Probably a passing school of little fish.

"Would you like to go out in the boat?" It was Arlan! Shelley clambered up the rocks.

"I thought it was bad luck to take girls out fishing," she said.

"We're not going fishing," Arlan explained. "I did that all day yesterday. We're going sightseeing. Anyhow, the girls do go out sometimes nowadays. But it's hard work, hauling nets and trawl. And—well," he said pointedly, "there's no head on most of the boats."

Shelley laughed. "Can I bring anything in the way of food?"

"Oh, no, Mum packed us a picnic."

Since Sentinel Head had no harbour or wharf of its own, the Brocks moored their trawler at a neighboring town, bringing their catch there, where it was collected and taken to one of the fish plants in Port Huyett. Shelley loved the place and pleaded with

Vernon to drive out in the evenings to watch the little boats coming in from the sea and back to port. She was fascinated by the unloading of the catch and the tidying up of the boats for the next run. Walking out on the wharf, she had learned how to stay out of the way of the ropes and the men themselves. It was traditionally a man's world, and she hadn't been surprised to discover that a superstition went along with it.

Shelley, with some lip biting, now negotiated the slippery iron ladder that went straight down to the first boat lying alongside the wharf. Following Arlan, who walked casually from boat to boat, she tried not to look down into the water as she stepped across the upper decks. In fact, the boats were astonishingly steady and hardly rocked at all under her feet. When they reached the *Drusilla J.*, Arlan jumped aboard, and Shelley, following, eased herself down onto the deck below. He disappeared into the little wheelhouse, and Shelley, not knowing exactly what to do, sat on the green-painted hatch cover and watched the water running up and down the scuppers as the boat responded to the waves. The trawler spelled *work*, not pleasure. She knew that Axel took care of his craft and gear, that he had a reputation for keeping a clean boat, but it still wasn't exactly a yacht.

"Don't you put your hand on that pipe, now, Shelley; it gets red hot." Shelley edged over to the other side of the hatch. In a stormy sea how could the men keep from lurching into the pipe?

"We're going out to sea," Arlan explained. "Way out. We're going to pass by Sentinel Head, and I have to stay out of the way of the shoals. I figured on rounding Crag Island so you can see where the Brocks came from."

The engine started with a roar. "We can't talk over this," Arlan shouted out the door. They chugged out the harbour.

From the sea, the land looked different. The houses perched a lot more precariously on the harbour edges than Shelley had imagined. They were like great birds that had flown in from the sea and alighted for a little while until they took off again. The land had always seemed so permanent, so stable, but all at once it seemed that the sea was forever and the things on the land of short duration. The shores were more jagged than she had realized and the spits and fingers of land much narrower. Sentinel Head, the whole headland, was almost insignificant; it was so tiny and frail. Arlan, as they passed, pointed vigorously toward the shore, and Shelley saw with a shock that they were passing her house, her rocks. It was hard to believe that she occupied so tiny a part of the land.

They headed toward Crag Island, the one Shelley could see from her kitchen window. It lay westward of Sentinel Head, and she'd often wondered about it. A stormy stretch of sea separated it from its natural mainland, a finger of land called Hebron Cove. At one time the two must have been connected, before the lowland between was finally breached by the sea. In the same way the outer reaches of Sentinel Head would someday separate, and the sea would flood in. As they neared Crag Island, she looked curiously at its emerging details.

There was no human life on it, none that Shelley could see anyway. She thought she might have glimpsed a sheep. The sea broke against the rocky shores, and the waves leaped up high clefts, gnawing at the island edges. It was a wild place, desolate, its trees gnarled and broken, clawed by the wind.

"We came from there," Arlan yelled from the engine house. Shelley nodded. She knew that Arlan's family way back, in the days of sail—along with some of the other families on Sentinel Head as well as Hebron Cove—had lived on Crag Island, where they were closer to the open ocean. Gasoline motors had allowed them to move to the mainland. But the roots of the people had been planted in a wild, hard place. She looked at the strip of sea separating Crag Island from the headland. Dru had told her a story about one of Arlan's ancestors, maybe his great great-grandmother. She was coming across from the island in an open boat, and it had capsized. Her young husband had drowned in the icy water, but her long skirt had ballooned up, keeping her afloat until she could be rescued. She later remarried, and from that marriage had come Arlan's family. Shelley looked at the water again and shivered. No wonder no one told Axel what to do; no wonder Arlan made up his own mind.

They moored in shallower water off the island and ate their picnic.

"Fishing's a hard life, isn't it?" Shelley commented.

"It's all we know, though. If the government puts us all on floating factories, as they want to, it's the end of our way of life. The fishermen are fighting it. I want to do something else with my life, though. I don't intend to get caught." He peered inside his sandwich, unjustifiably suspicious of his mother.

"That's why you're going into the Coast Guard?"

"Well, I'm no teacher or anything, so college isn't for me even if we could afford it. But I can get what I want, the technical training, if I stay in the service. I've got it all planned out." He got up and started toward the wheelhouse.

"I want to take you around the island," he said. "Give you another taste of the open ocean. I hope you're not seasick," he teased.

"It's the first time I've ever been out in a boat," she told him.

"Shelley!" Arlan gasped. "Gosh, I never thought! Are you scared—or anything?"

"I *like* being out in a boat," she reassured him. "Really, I do." And she did, a gift from Conrad Joyner, her fisherman grandfather.

The trip took longer than Shelley had expected. On the seaward side Crag Island had huge inlets, coves, and protruding arms, even a lovely, never-used beach of white sand. Arlan followed the contours of the shore closely, allowing Shelley time to get a feel for the place.

The long, slow swells were exciting. Shelley liked the roll, and in spite of Arlan's anxiety, she wasn't seasick at all. It was a wonderful day, and she was sorry when the autumn sun dropped early in the sky. As they chugged homeward, she watched the shags, the cormorants, with a feeling of kinship. The birds were flying in straight, no-nonsense lines, from the mainland to their roosts on the island trees.

She'd been happier, more at home, at sea in the boat with Arlan than she'd been anywhere in her whole life. She turned and looked back at Crag Island, its profile strong against the softening sky. She had no family claim to it, but nothing on earth could stop her from taking away a piece of it for her own or, for that matter, could stop her from leaving a piece of herself on its receding shore. There was no one to stop her from claiming Sentinel Head as home either. Sometimes, like the seabirds, you had to stake out a little bit of territory for your own. And fight for it, she thought sadly. Fight to keep it.

Chapter 6

SEPTEMBER SPILLED OVER INTO OCTOBER, JUST barely, but even so, Shelley could feel the difference. The year was dying, of course, but it was going out in a lot of glory and happiness. It was the same way at home.

Shelley wouldn't let herself think about the dying; she couldn't. Everything else was so unexpectedly right; she could almost convince herself that Vernon had been wrong, that he would settle here and thrive. There had already been such unbelievable changes. Why not a miracle?

All month Vernon had been taking Catherine places. Astonishing! Catherine's lifelong plaint was that he never went anywhere. Shelley looked out her classroom window one morning and saw the two of them strolling across the beach in front of the school. Getting Catherine on her feet for a hike was remarkable enough, but both of them would stop from time to time and pick up bits of sea driftings to examine, a new world.

They had begun to explore the various necks and coves up and down the coast, taking picnic lunches with them, as Shelley discovered from the remains when she got home. Catherine had fallen in love with one of the harbours. They'd drive there, to the edge of the government wharf, and sit for hours, watching the boats and the fishermen come and go. Many of the houses surrounding the little harbour had window boxes of bright flowers, and Vernon undertook to put together a box for Catherine. He'd never seemed particularly handy with tools; he hadn't had to do much carpentry at the various apartments, of course, but he came up with a really decent window box. Catherine got busy and painted it.

"Why don't we fill it, and you can get it ready for next spring?" Vernon said. "After I fix the windows, the house will look like one of those in your favorite town."

Shelley didn't want to wait for next spring. Catherine had a thing about plants. It was not that she nursed them tenderly, out of love for them. She seemed to need them for some reason other than nurture. She bossed them around and bullied them into growing. Even her pruning was rough, transmitting a message to shape up or ship out. Her treatment of the luxuriant ivies and coleus plants that brightened the kitchen made Shelley uneasy, but *anything* that was important to Catherine had to be noted, and if Catherine wanted plants for her window box, Shelley was minded to do something about it.

On the way to and from school each day, the bus passed by a roadside garden, now a wild jumble of fall flowers. Janet laughed when Shelley asked about it.

"Oh well," Janet said, "he gets fish guts from the wharf and lets them rot in buckets. He pours the brew all over the garden, and the flowers bloom like crazy, but I swear to God, they smell like fish."

"Would he let me have a couple plants?" Shelley asked on the way home one day.

When Janet answered, "Oh, my dear, he'll give you the whole garden!" Shelley got off the bus and walked the three miles home with a sack of chrysanthemums. Catherine was delighted.

"That was really nice of you, Shelley!" she exclaimed and hurried outside to plant the flowers in her new window box.

"We ought to do whatever we can do to get her used to this place. Before—" Vernon said and hesitated. "Things will be—safer—for you if she kind of takes root."

There wouldn't be a miracle, not any. Shelley turned away, preferring to fight her battles in private.

"I wonder if it will last," she asked finally, when she was sure her voice wouldn't tremble. "Catherine taking root, I mean." Vernon didn't answer. There wasn't any answer. After Vernon was—gone—Catherine was perfectly capable of snatching Shelley from her newfound home, with no more feeling than she had when she switched plants from pot to pot. And he knew it as well as she did.

As the days passed, the settling in seemed to go even more easily because of Arlan: He helped. Once a week he solemnly presented the Joyners with a fish. When Shelley insisted on cleaning it herself, he showed up with a Jack the Ripper.

"For your birthday," he teased her. "When is it?"

"Sweet sixteen," she informed him. "Not till later."

He kept on showing up. Catherine, after some initial coolness to him, began to thaw out. She even became coquettish, which Shelley found both grotesque and pathetic. She worried about what Arlan would think, but he showed considerable understanding of Catherine. He teased her, seeming to know instinctively when to steady her, when to withdraw completely.

"This is a hard place for your mother, I believe," he said once as he walked Shelley home.

"In some ways," Shelley responded. "But she seems a lot happier here. They both do."

"How about you?" Arlan asked. "Do you like it here?"

"Your folks have been so nice to me, Arlan," she said.

"Oh, come on, Shelley!" Arlan said, laughing. "Just my *folks*?"

"No," she answered firmly, "not just them. You, too."

Shelley thought she might as well let Arlan know she cared about him. If, as people said, Arlan was going to be reluctant making up his mind about a girl, meaning Shelley Joyner, that same Shelley Joyner had better help him out.

Just the same, it was apparent that Arlan was in no hurry. When they were together, they had a lot of fun, going to hamburger places, and, when Arlan had time, sort of batting around. Nothing romantic. Shelley talked Arlan into visiting a local museum. He'd lived all his life there, but he'd never been in it. It turned out to be mostly a history of fishing in Nova Scotia, and Shelley learned a lot from Arlan as he got interested in the displays. They didn't go out on the Head together again, though Shelley went often by herself. The kids at school teased them about going together, and Shelley thought Arlan was deliberately staying away from the Head, playing it cool. It was all right with her. She didn't want to get overinvolved—yet. There was too much to do at home, too much to worry about.

Sometimes Shelley walked down the road to spend an evening with the Brocks. Arlan was bogged down in essay writing for his last English course, and he was more than grateful for her help. He talked easily enough, about fishing and everyday things, but writing was an agony for him. The words would not come, and when he finally got something down on paper, it was lifeless, couched in a stilted prose that didn't sound like him at all. Just the physical act of setting pen to paper was hard for him. His fingers were too big and stiff, the pen was too small, and his hands were chapped.

Arlan fished on the weekends, and though he hated it, in off hours he baited trawl for his father at the harbour fish shed. Good money could be made if you were willing to sit there and hook frozen mackerel onto the barbed trawl coils, and some of the kids did it. Arlan wouldn't bait trawl for money, he told Shelley, but the chore fell to him because he was the youngest member of the Brock team. His hands, already raw from handling the frozen mackerel, cracked in the icy seawater when he went out fishing.

Shelley hated to see his sore hands. "You need some of those great big fishing mittens, like those we saw in the museum. The kind they used to shrink in saltwater." Arlan looked down at his hands.

"We still use them, Shelley," he said. "And lobstering's coming up. I wish you'd knit me some."

Nothing had ever given Shelley such a sense of pleasure—and possession—in her whole life. She learned the knitting pattern and got the wool from Dru, but she found she was knitting Arlan right into the tight rows of the mittens.

When Shelley wasn't visiting the Brocks, she walked further up the road to Janet's. She particularly liked Janet's granny-mum, who showed up at suppertimes with casseroles and a succession of cakes and cookies. Janet's mother came home late and tired from the Harbour Gull to a whole tableful of smaller Crawfords—Janet was the oldest. The father spent long weeks at sea, working the draggers. Things were not as comfortable here as at the Brocks', but it was a noisy, exciting kitchen, and Shelley on occasion joined the others at tea and homework around the table. By now she and Janet were fast friends.

"Why don't you walk up to my place?" Shelley asked and then warned her, "It's a lot—well, *quieter* than your house." Janet laughed.

"Well, I guess," she said. But she came and immediately disarmed Catherine. In a few minutes they were chatting away like old chums. It didn't seem fair, somehow. Watching Catherine's spirited response to Janet's joshing, Shelley thought of the years she'd wished for just this kind of give and take, but it had never happened. Why? She didn't know. How had Janet so easily slid into a place that should have been hers?

One evening Shelley answered a knock at the kitchen door and found Dru standing a little shyly on the stoop. She had come to invite the three Joyners to supper on Shelley's birthday. Vernon and Catherine looked at each other in surprise. Unused to invitations, they didn't seem to know what to say or how to say it, so Shelley did it for them.

"Lovely!" she said. "We'll be there, all three of us."

Shelley thought she might have a fight on her hands to get them to go, but both Vernon and Catherine were all dressed and ready when she got home from school. It turned out to be a real party, just the two families, the Brocks and Joyners. There was a cake, of course. Dru had baked and decorated it herself. Shelley had an idea the three men in Dru's family were a poor audience for pink decorated cakes. At any rate, Dru had made the most of this opportunity, and the cake caused a sensation.

"How come I never got a cake like that?" Arlan demanded. Dru looked at him in amazement.

"She always bakes a cake, all right," Arlan amended hastily. "But she settles for plain old chocolate frosting."

"You should be glad she doesn't decorate your cakes with fishhooks," Shelley pointed out. She looked over at Catherine and wondered what she was thinking. Did she care that somebody else's mother had baked a birthday cake for her? It had happened before, of course, almost every year, in fact. She'd celebrated all her last birthdays with Jeanne-Louise. But the way things were going, the three of them acting almost like a family, suppose Dru hadn't invited them all to supper, would Catherine for once have baked her a cake? However, Catherine's face showed no expression, certainly not wistfulness or regret. Better just erase the thought.

"Happy birthday," Arlan said as she blew out the candles. "Now you can get married without permission." Shelley was in the middle of a laugh—who in the world was she going to marry?—when Catherine burst out, "She'd better not!" The silence that followed was embarrassing, and Shelley turned her face away. When things were going so well, why did

Catherine *have* to be so bitchy? What was bugging her anyway?

Shelley caught Arlan's eye. Had he seen how mad she was? She hoped not. He gave her a quick smile and said easily, "Did you hear what your mother said? You're going to have to wait!" Then he grinned openly at her, and Shelley felt her cheeks sting with heat.

"A lot of the girls around here marry young, Catherine," Dru said. "I was only sixteen myself. I rather think Janet and Craig are fixing to get married, after Christmas sometime. Granny-mum seems to think so anyhow, and she has a feeling for that sort of thing."

"Well, sixteen's too young," Catherine said flatly. "For anyone." There was an uncomfortable silence.

"Janet's a nice girl," Vernon commented, peaceably changing the subject. "I like her. She had us all laughing the other night."

"Dad used to call her Dumplings and Apple Pie," Arlan observed. "One of the nicer names he's come up with for the girls around here."

"I shudder to think what he calls me," Shelley said, relieved to get off the subject of early marriage and onto Janet.

"I don't call the girls anything," Axel said bluntly. "Not anymore. Arlan fixed that. He said whatever he brought home he damn well intended to keep, and he'd do the naming himself." He laughed heartily, and everyone, including Arlan, joined him, but even while she laughed, Shelley felt herself blushing, and at that she saw Catherine turn into a thundercloud.

On the way home, Catherine snapped, "Shelley, you'd better watch it with Arlan, or you'll get caught and find yourself getting married at sixteen, too. I'll bet anything Janet gets pregnant before Christmas."

"I don't think so," Shelley stated irritably. "And it wouldn't be any business of yours if she did. And for your information, I'm not about to get pregnant."

"Stay out of her life, Catherine," Vernon said in weariness. "So *you* got caught. It doesn't mean Shelley's going to."

"I've got a program I want to watch." Catherine quickened her steps, and reaching the house, went inside, slamming the door behind her.

"Let's drive into town and watch the harbour lights for a little while," Vernon suggested, fishing the car keys out of his pocket. "It's such a nice evening." Shelley, surprised and pleased, got into the car with him, and they drove to Port Huyett and out onto the harbour wharf. It was dark, clear, and the reflection of the shore lights made patterns on the water and lit up the boats rocking at anchor alongside the wharf.

"Are you warm enough?" she asked. Vernon had already begun to wear his winter jacket, but even so he shivered a lot, vulnerable to even the mildest wind. He nodded absently.

"You know Billy's not my child," he said quietly after a moment. "I never knew who the father was.

I don't think Catherine knows, either. There were several choices, I gather," he added, without apparent rancor.

"Then why—" Shelley started to say and stopped hastily.

"Why did she pick me?" Vernon finished the sentence. "She hated her mother, and she ran away from home after her father died. She had a job at the factory; that's where I met her. There were men around her all the time. When she got pregnant, she had to quit work—she had to be on her feet all day, you see." He stopped. Shelley turned to him a little impatiently. She knew all this.

"Catherine was beautiful when she was a young girl," Vernon said. "Really beautiful. She married me—out of desperation, probably," he said with a short laugh. "You've got to understand, though, Shelley, that she was really beautiful."

Shelley nodded. She'd seen pictures. Sometimes when Catherine came home flushed from the beauty parlor, she was still pretty.

"She never really grew up," Vernon said. "She doted on her father. She never got over looking for him, in me or any other man. I didn't know her mother well. I only saw her once. You were with me. Do you remember that? Catherine and she had been at each other's throats for years. Jealousy, I suppose. The father gave Catherine everything she wanted. Everything *I* couldn't give her."

"But you brought up Billy," Shelley said slowly.

"I did the best I could with him," Vernon replied. "Catherine was awfully young. She wasn't much of a mother—always after a good time. I expect she feels a lot of guilt about everything. I know that she and her mother had bitter words before she took off. Catherine has a cruel tongue. She broke with the rest of the family, and she's never seen her mother again, never even talked to her. I hate to think what passed between them. You're right at the age where she ran away, Shelley, and I suppose all Catherine's old hate and guilt are stirred up again."

"She's always said I was a mistake," Shelley said. "I've always wondered if she really liked me."

"I didn't ever think you were a mistake." Vernon smiled. "You've been a good daughter, Shelley, and it's going to be hard for you, dealing with Catherine. I know that. All you can do is cope the best you can. You won't be able to change her." He sighed and then bent over to start the car. "I like Arlan," he said gently.

"Vernon—" Shelley said in desperation. Still with his hand on the key, he turned to her.

"Let's not talk about it, Shelley. We'll know when it comes. I've been to the clinic, and they're going to want me in the hospital soon for tests. I've been to see an attorney and made what arrangements I can for the two of you. But I'd rather not spoil our time together." He smiled and started the car.

He'd been pretty heroic. He'd been caring for her for a long time, and she'd never even noticed it. She'd never given him any real affection, not the kind she saw all the time at the Brocks'. But suddenly he was a father, a real one, and it was almost too late. She needed him. She needed more time to settle in. There was so much to do, so much to be said, so many problems. Her lips trembled, and she turned her head aside.

There was Catherine. She was going to be a terrible problem. Shelley could try to forge a new relationship with her father before it was too late, but Catherine would be in the way. She could be in the way of her relationship with Arlan, too. No matter what happened, almost certainly Catherine was going to be in the way of her new life in Sentinel Head, and she might easily destroy it altogether.

Chapter 7

ONE DAY, AT THE END OF OCTOBER, SHELLEY CAME home from school and discovered both her parents gummed up with tile cement, sitting exhausted on the kitchen floor, laying tiles.

"Why didn't you buy the self-adhering kind?" Shelley asked, dropping her books and getting ready to pitch in and help.

"These were a lot less expensive, Shelley," explained Vernon patiently. "Probably some job lot left over." Shelley nodded. She could have figured it out for herself.

Catherine was only too glad to turn the job over to Shelley, and without a word she disappeared into the bathroom to clean up. Vernon continued to sit on the floor without moving.

"I'll finish the tile," Shelley said uneasily. She'd never seen anyone look so weary. He finally got up and sat limply in the rocker.

"I don't know what I'm going to do, Shelley," he said. "I'm just so tired—I haven't the strength, and I've got to get at those windows."

"It doesn't matter about the windows, Vernon," Shelley reassured him. She looked up at him. "Honestly."

"I've set my mind to it," he persisted. "You've always called this an old blind house. I can't leave you here like this."

Shelley, stabbed, spun around and knelt at the rocker. "I'll do the windows for you," she pleaded. "I'll find out how to do them."

Vernon shook his head. Then clumsily, covering his face with one hand and turning away in shame, he began to cry, deep shuddering sobs.

Shelley got off the school bus the next morning and headed straight for the principal's office. She was about to confront the lioness in her den, and she didn't dare think about it.

Mrs. Luddington looked up from a pile of papers on her desk and took off her heavy glasses. "Shelley Joyner?" she asked.

Shelley, startled, was immediately off balance. Why in the world had Mrs. Luddington bothered to find out her name or remember it if she had? No one in No-Hope had ever done such a thing.

"I want to transfer to the vocational school," Shelley said, more belligerently than she had intended. She had to corral her strength, had to wrest back the initiative from Mrs. Luddington. "I have to learn how to make windows," she added, ready for a fight.

Mrs. Luddington looked neither surprised nor particularly combative. "Why windows?" she asked with interest and even a little amusement. Then a quick frown passed over her face, and she looked out the office window for a moment, studying the sweep of beach and the sea rolling in.

"I ran into Axel Brock the other day, Shelley," she commented finally. "He told me a little about you. Your father's not well, I understand."

"No," Shelley answered. She was back on the defensive. As Janet had said, this lady was some tough and also one jump ahead of the game.

"Perhaps you are undertaking some project your father is unable to do?"

Shelley gulped. "The front windows," she had to say. "He . . . he isn't strong enough to put them in, and we can't afford to buy them either. I have to make them." And if Mrs. Luddington had in mind, as she might, that either she or Vernon would go begging to the Brocks for help, she had another think coming. Shelley really resented Mrs. Luddington, as she sat there thinking, her eyes turned downward on, but apparently not seeing, the pile of papers in front of her.

"Well," she said, looking up at last. "I'm not going to let you give up the academic program here. It may be valuable to you in a way you don't see right now." Shelley stiffened in anger. "But Mr. Goodman, out at the vocational school, teaches carpentry, and

65

he might be able to help you," she continued calmly. "He would probably enjoy a project of this kind. Let me see if I can't arrange to have you go out and talk to him." She smiled briefly.

Shelley picked up her backpack of books from the floor, where she had deposited them. When you get all your armor ready for a fight and there isn't one, she thought, you feel sort of wobbly.

"The Brocks would do it for you in a minute, I know," Mrs. Luddington said, "but it wouldn't do right now. I suspect you *need* to do this for your father." She stood up, dismissing Shelley. "Good luck," she said.

The following Friday found Shelley at the vocational school, sitting beside Mr. Goodman's desk.

"I don't get many girls out here," he said, taking off his glasses and blowing a film of sawdust off the lens. Then he put them back on and looked sharply at Shelley. "Especially girls gung ho to make windows. You live in the Reedie place, I understand."

Shelley nodded. Word got around awfully fast in these parts.

"Reedie—I knew him and his wife very well, by the way. They built your house around themselves, bit by bit. He was a good workman, and that's a well-built house. But his wife died suddenly, and Reedie never finished it out. He moved into the kitchen and the little room under the stair. Boarded everything else up. He lived there for years, alone. Some idiot moved in after he died and put up that ramshackle shed for a bathroom."

"I'll build a new bathroom later," Shelley said

grimly. "But I'd better start with the windows. My father . . ."

"Mrs. Luddington told me about him," Mr. Goodman interrupted. "Now listen, Shelley. No one builds windows these days. They haven't for years. Windows come in standard sizes, and you simply frame them in. One of the Brocks could help you do that."

"But I can't afford to buy windows. They're expensive, and I need two," Shelley explained.

Mr. Goodman nodded. "Lots of people around here have replaced their original windows with picture windows and bays. No one throws things away. Those old windows and casings are stored in barns and sheds all over the area."

"I . . . see," Shelley said. "Then all I'd have to do is fit them in and trim them out? Could I get them *out* of an old, abandoned house—if I can find an old, abandoned house?"

"Well, I'd suggest you get some help," Mr. Goodman said dryly. "Someone with strong arms. What size windows do you need? Do you know?"

"I wrote down the measurements. I took off the inside boards and measured."

"Good. Well, see what you can do by yourself. Ask around. If you can't locate any, let me know. The finishing out is not very difficult. You might enjoy learning how to do it," he suggested. "More fun than cooking."

"I can do that, too," Shelley pointed out.

"I bet. Now I want to hear from you. Reedie would be mighty surprised to know a girl was finishing up his windows. Pleased, though." He nodded.

Shelley hitched a ride back to Sentinel Head with one of the school board maintenance trucks. The afternoon was already half over, and she had something more important on her mind than going back to the high school. Slipping into the house, she mumbled an excuse to Vernon about needing his tape line, and then she made for the Head and Jaimie's old farmhouse. Sheep didn't have to have windows that went up and down, and she did.

Jaimie probably wasn't about. She'd have to confront him sooner or later about the windows, but it would be better to have the facts at hand. She followed the truck tracks to the sheep barn.

The old house sat on stone foundations, but the ground floor had long since rotted away. The earth had built up inside, and the sheep came and went by the doorway, which was gnawed by time and enlarged by the crowding of the flock. Jaimie had constructed racks for supplies above the reach of the sheep, and parts of the area had been binned or fenced off for various purposes, lambing or perhaps shearing. Shelley didn't know enough about sheep to decipher the geography of the place. It smelled earthy inside, not unpleasant, and underfoot, to her surprise, it was not too bad at all. The sea air blew straight through, of course, keeping the barn relatively fresh. All the downstairs windows (and casings, Shelley noted) were long gone.

She examined the remains of the rough stairway

that led to the loft. The lower part was missing, eaten away by rot, or perhaps Jaimie had even hacked it away. Sheep climbed rocks; maybe they climbed stairs, though the picture of it in her mind made her chuckle. She reached up and tested the strength of the remaining staircase; it seemed firm enough. It was precarious going, but in the end she got herself onto the stairs by climbing various projections on the side wall and none too gracefully heaving herself upward.

The upstairs, the loft, was empty, apparently undisturbed for a long time. It was a chilly day, and up there the wind really howled and whistled. Shelley thought what a fearful place it would be in a storm. Still, as she had expected, the view was spectacular, and she spent a little time taking it in before she began to examine the windows. To her delight, the gable windows were the right size, and there were two of them.

She got herself down the staircase more easily than she had gotten herself up, gravity being a strong aid and succor. Not wanting Jaimie to catch her trespassing in the sheep barn, in case he came out to the Head earlier than usual for some reason, she hurried back across the truck path and crawled over the gate.

So far, so good, she thought. Maybe it would ease Vernon's mind to have the job done, give him a sense of completion. Catherine had been pleased with the kitchen floor. "It's some better," she'd said, mocking the local talk. Maybe new windows would make her feel even more at home, heel her more deeply into the soil.

Old Jaimie

Jaimie, out of old loyalty to Conrad Joyner and nothing else, drove his truck clear across the island to Digby, where Nellie, a cousin of Conrad Joyner, still lived. He hadn't been in touch with her for years, though at one point in his youth, when she was visiting Conrad, he'd been sweet on her. Nothing had come of it, and both of them had married in due course, she a Fundy man. Through a relative of Nellie's late husband, Jaimie located her, an even more painful exercise than he'd expected, the digging up of old acquaintances and a past he'd so long stowed away. He hadn't thought to call Nellie, and it took her at least an hour of feather settling before he could get her down to business.

"Why yes, Conrad had a son!" she exclaimed. "Conrad wrote me years ago. Just stay right there!" She hastened off into another part of the house and rustled, while Jaimie, who had been herded into the sitting room in honor of the occasion, endured, as out of place in the crocheted doilies as the ram of the flock himself.

" 'Dear Cousin Nellie,' " Nellie read, and then turned the letter over. "Let me see, this is dated 1950. From Sidney. I put the date down myself, when I *received it. You know, it's the only letter I ever had from him. He died in 1952, when the little feller was only nine year old. 'Dear Cousin Nellie,' " she continued at last:*

> *"Been a long time since I heard from you or any of the folks. I been working in the mines here, it's dirty work underground, but these times it's work anyhow. Been thinking about all of you there, wondering what's happened to you, been missing the sea too though after the ship gone down and I saw Martin Brock blown up that way seemed I never wanted to go out again. Nellie, you never wrote me what happened to Jaimie Wenloch.*

"I did, too," Nellie argued. "I . . ."

"Go on with the letter," Jaimie said.

> *"Mary Sue is well and sends regards and the lad would too if he knew about you. He's a frail little fellow, wish he could breathe sea air, maybe it would do him some good.*

"And it's signed 'Love from Conrad, Mary Sue and Vernon.' Vernon! There! That was the name. Vernon. I believe the child had measles and fever. He was terribly sick, and they almost lost him."

"What happened to the mother?" Jaimie asked.

"Well, she was left without much, and I think she had a real struggle. She went back to her hometown and ran a little grocery store there and raised the boy. Vernon went into the factory without finishing his schooling, and he married some girl he

met there. Mary Sue didn't get along with her; I know that much. Mary Sue's been gone some time now, and whether Vernon had children, I don't know. I lost track of them after Mary Sue died."

"Well, thanks, Nellie. I have to be going now," Jaimie said, rising with effort from the festooned chair.

"You'll never such!" exclaimed Nellie. "An old man like you crossing the island twice in a day! You'll stay the night, and no argument from you. Anyhow, I want to know what this is all about."

It was November, with a driving rain outside, and cold. Nellie had been cooking something toothsome in the kitchen.

"I'd take it kindly," he said gruffly, and sank back into the nest of crochet.

Jaimie left in the morning and took his time going back. He stopped briefly at home in Port Huyett and then drove out to the moor to check his sheep. It had been good to visit with Nellie, and it was a relief, in a way, to have settled the matter of Vernon Joyner. He'd have to tell Axel what he'd discovered. Unless his mother had told him about Conrad, her husband's boyhood friend, Axel wouldn't have been likely to make the connection with the name.

Jaimie liked Axel. The Brocks had always lived somewhat apart. Axel was like his father, Martin, in that, and he'd heard that Arlan was much like Axel. They made up their minds and stuck to things, neither asking for community opinion nor mindful of what came back to them by way of gossip or hearsay. They'd been a good fishing team, the Brock men, and

Axel was going to miss Arlan if he got himself into the Coast Guard. Old Jaimie had heard Arlan was sweet on the Joyner girl, and he'd had to churn up a lot of crustiness to mask his enjoyment of this news. He'd kept an eye on the girl, wondering about her relationship to Conrad. She reminded him of a Lunenburg schooner, sturdy but with a grace as well.

Well, he'd have to go visit Vernon, too, though he'd heard the man wasn't doing at all well. It would be an effort. He was tired. As he parked at the sheep barn, he glanced back across the moor. Then he frowned. The Joyner girl was bearing down on him, running straight afore the wind and heading directly for the truck. He had to wait. He climbed down from the cab to meet her.

Conrad Joyner's blue eyes bore into him again.

"I need something of yours," the girl said. "I have to have two windows out of your house."

Chapter 8

SHELLEY HADN'T EXPECTED QUITE THE REACTION she got to her demand. Jaimie was plainly thunderstruck. Of course, people didn't usually go around demanding windows out of somebody else's house, and he was within his rights to show some feeling. But then she saw his tightened-up old face relax and crinkle into amusement.

"Well now," he said mildly. "Which windows were you planning to take?"

"The ones in the gable. They're the same size as our front windows. I went up and measured them."

Jaimie's eyebrows arched. "You should never have gone up that stair," he scolded. "It could have let you down."

"Well, I had to," Shelley explained. "We live in the . . . the Reedie place." She pointed, and Jaimie nodded without looking. "I have to get those windows in before . . ." She stopped and looked into his face. *Please!* she begged silently. Jaimie waited, and something about his waiting reassured her. There wasn't much about life that would astonish Jaimie, she thought.

"Before my father dies," she finished. "He's getting a lot weaker, and he can't do it himself."

Jaimie looked off to sea for a moment, a gesture obviously familiar, for it seemed a part of him. It was Shelley's turn to wait. When he turned back, his face was almost gentle. How many people had ever seen it that way?

"I knew your grandfather," he said. "Conrad Joyner. I fished with him, see, along with Axel's father. We were all three in the war together. Your grandfather left Sentinel Head to marry, and he never made it back. I didn't know till yesterday he had a son." Shelley, her head whirling, stared speechless at the old man.

"So your father brought you home, did he?" he asked sadly.

* * *

"Conrad Joyner!" Axel exclaimed, hitting his head with the palm of his hand. "But Mum used to talk about him! I'd clean forgotten—never put the names together at all."

"I didn't know there had ever been Joyners around here," Dru commented, puzzled. "I know there are some on the Fundy side. I never heard the name around here."

"I even have a cousin over there," Shelley announced, proud to claim a relative on Nova Scotia soil.

"I *told* you she belonged," Arlan pointed out.

Axel continued to look disturbed. "Now why wouldn't your father have said something?"

"I haven't been home yet to ask," Shelley explained. "I just wanted to tell you folks about it." She meant Arlan.

Axel shook his head. "I don't understand it at all."

"Vernon's like that," Shelley said. "He hates asking for help."

"Seems like it runs in the family," Arlan observed. "Pigheadedness. Some people I know won't let anyone else clean their fish, even if it is a man's job."

Dru snorted. "Some people I know actually give a girl a ripper for her birthday," she pointed out. "It doesn't seem to show an awful lot of imagination."

"Anyhow," Shelley said, laughing comfortably. *I told you she belonged* had had to be the nicest thing she'd ever heard. "Anyhow, I'm about to ask for some help. Mr. Goodman out at the vocational school told me to look around for some windows for the front of the house, and I asked Old Jaimie if I could have two of his."

"Old Jaimie!" chorused three voices at once.

"How'd you get out to Goodman?" Arlan asked, curious.

"Vernon really wants those windows in, and— well, he can't do it himself anymore. I thought if I could transfer to the vocational school, I could learn to make them, but Mrs. Luddington wouldn't let me. She sent me out there, though."

"You don't make windows," Axel said bluntly.

"That's what Mr. Goodman said. He told me to look for some. I was going to take them from Jaimie's upstairs, but he says he's got a couple stored away, and he's going to drop them off."

"Gosh, Shelley!" Arlan looked his admiration.

"I'll be damned. Old Jaimie!" Axel shook his head again. "I'll just walk out there. I don't want him trying to lift those things himself."

"Jaimie said he wanted to talk to you anyhow," Shelley explained. "He went clear over to Digby to ask about Vernon."

Axel took his jacket from the coat pegs. "Arlan, you and Shelley go and measure for trim. I may have enough in the shed, but if I don't, you can pick up what we need tomorrow. The weather's due to hold. We'll get them in right away."

Vernon's reaction to the windows was typical— an alarmed series of protests: He didn't want to impose, he didn't need help, he'd manage by himself.

76

"Oh, come on, Vernon," Arlan said easily. "You've got two strong backs here, and besides," he gave Shelley a comic look, "it's neighborly. I've been trying to ram that into your daughter's head."

Arlan knew about framing windows. He'd helped build an extension to his own house, and he wasn't making any big thing about framing in two windows. On reconsidering, Shelley was awfully glad Mrs. Luddington and Mr. Goodman between them had fouled up her noble plan for leaving high school. This way was a lot more sensible, neighborly, whatever.

"Vernon, did you know Old Jaimie fished with your father and Axel's, too?" Shelley asked, in between measuring and jotting.

Vernon shook his head. "I was just a little chap when he died. I remembered the name of the town he came from. Sentinel Head. He was always homesick for it. It sounded right—for us." He smiled shyly. "I'd like to talk to Old Jaimie."

"He's coming to see you," Shelley said.

"Hey, Catherine!" Arlan called, and Catherine walked in from the kitchen. As Vernon weakened and their outings became fewer, she'd gone back to the TV, listlessly, Shelley thought.

"Mum says she has some drapes we used before we put in the bay window, if you'd like to have them," Arlan said. "This house is going to look some good when we get finished with it."

"It's nice of you and Axel to help," Catherine said. "You folks are being really decent to us."

"We have an interest," Arlan pointed out. "We're into planting roots around here."

"Shelley, maybe," Catherine said. "She's good at planting roots. I don't know about me."

The new windows were wonderful. Shelley couldn't believe how the house had brightened. Catherine had the drapes all hung one day when Shelley got home from school, and to Shelley's amusement, she had moved the TV in from the kitchen.

"I'm tired of sitting in there," she complained. "Same thing every day."

Catherine and Vernon were doing a lot more sitting, in any case. Shelley would find them huddled by the stove when she came home. It was almost as if Vernon's last project had been completed with the windows and he was letting go. When the doctor at the medical clinic in town called and said they had an opening at the hospital, he seemed almost relieved. He handed Shelley the household money.

"Take care of things," he said. Shelley, with a concerned look at Catherine's suddenly stiffened figure, but not wanting to make a scene, reluctantly took the money. She'd try to work it out later.

Arlan drove all three of them to the hospital and afterward took Catherine and Shelley back to their empty house.

"Be sure to call on us," Arlan urged, taking Shelley by the shoulders and shaking her a little to make his point. "Don't be pigheaded." Then he left, and Shelley and Catherine were alone, face to face with the future.

"Well," said Catherine, "now that it's on the line, and I guess you know that it is, the two of us are going to have to learn how to live together."

Shelley looked at her in amazement. "But it's what I've been trying to do all along!" she exclaimed.

"You're just like Vernon," Catherine persisted. "You know that, don't you?"

"No, I don't," Shelley answered. Her stomach tightened. It was ridiculous. She and Vernon? "I don't know what you mean."

"Think it over," said Catherine roughly. "And by the way, since Vernon seems to have put you in charge of the exchequer, maybe you'd better start out by giving me bus fare for a while. If you think you can afford it," she added sarcastically. "I don't intend to sit around here all alone while you're in school."

"I'll take care of the grocery shopping. I can do it at noon, during the lunch hour," Shelley said calmly. She wasn't about to let Catherine know that her words had stung. "But you'll be wanting to visit Vernon. I presume," she couldn't help saying. Catherine didn't answer. Shelley laid money on the table. "There's money for lunches, too," she said. It was a reckless handling of the funds, but if Catherine was going to taunt her with Vernon's stinginess, she wasn't going to be miserly with Catherine's share of the money. She'd go without lunch herself first.

"How long have you known that Vernon was . . . so sick?" Shelley asked.

"Shelley, let me tell you something. It's been a long time, a lot longer than *you* have any idea." She took the little stack of bills and walked off to her room, closing the door. Shelley cleaned up the kitchen and, gathering her homework, climbed the stairs to her room.

She sat at her desk, studying the lines and scratches on the surface, tracing them absently with her finger, and trying to find some idea, some fragment of thought or reason, that would soften the sting of Catherine's words. In these last months, when it was almost too late, she'd learned to love her father, but no such chemistry was working with Catherine. She had honestly tried. But flower boxes, kitchen floors, and even front windows had not really done it. The idea that she and Vernon were much alike was plainly ridiculous and shouldn't have mattered anyhow, but whatever Catherine was looking for in her, she was obviously not providing, never had.

Increasingly Sentinel Head, for her, was home, but when Vernon died, how could she be sure she wouldn't lose everything at once, any hope of family, even the place she called home?

She would have to do better with Catherine; that's all. She'd promised herself she'd manage, she'd make a home, by herself if need be. She made the pledge all over again. Then she opened her history book and grimly dug into the assigned pages.

Vernon had been in the hospital for a week. Shelley walked over to visit him every day at lunch hour and even spent part of the afternoon one day when the old school boiler broke down and school had to be dismissed. It was then that she ran into a doctor just leaving Vernon's room.

"I'm Shelley Joyner," she explained. The doctor walked with her back down the hall to the lounge, and they both sat down. Shelley looked at the doctor, waiting for an answer to the question she didn't know how to ask.

"He has the body of an old man, Shelley," the doctor said. "Try to look at it that way. He just seems to have worn out early." He thought for a moment. "Your father said he went to work in a chemical factory when he was very young, when he was still almost a child."

Shelley nodded. "After his father died in the mines," she said. "They had a rough time of it, I think. They never had enough money. They moved back to my grandmother's hometown, and Vernon worked in the factory."

The doctor sighed. "Poor nutrition. Strain. He had rheumatic fever after the measles. He was probably never very strong."

"He's always worried about the air," Shelley volunteered.

The doctor looked thoughtful and finally said, "Your father told me *his* father had been a fisherman, and that he never really adjusted to the mining life. Some people just seem to need the sea air. They don't seem to thrive when they're away from it."

It was strange. Shelley liked the cold sea air herself. She found it bracing, but it was almost too much for Vernon. Axel had told her once that tomatoes and some trees couldn't grow on Sentinel Head. "Wind wilt," he called it, and she thought Vernon was like the plants.

"I guess he wanted . . . us . . . to thrive," Shelley said, and she felt her voice tremble, though she made an effort to control it. "That's probably why he brought us here."

"That's part of the answer. He hoped that Sentinel Head would be a caring place, I suspect." The doctor looked down at her. "It won't be very long, Shelley. Maybe only a few weeks. I think he'll be happier at home, with you and your mother. I want to keep him here for another week, though."

Shelley walked home with Janet the next day after school. Catherine hadn't been home afternoons for several days. She'd come home on the late bus and walk in from the trunk road. No explanation. But Shelley found the cold, empty house far from inviting, and she was glad to go home with Janet.

In honor of the occasion, Janet brewed a pot of tea, and they sat companionably out in the kitchen to drink it.

"Arlan said anything yet?" Janet asked amiably. Shelley shook her head. She didn't particularly want to talk about it. Janet chattered all the time, to everybody, with no malice whatsoever, but just the same, she could say more than you wanted her to.

"Didn't he ever go out with you?" Shelley asked. "I know he likes you."

Janet shook her head. "I'm not his type. I guess I was just born a homebody. Axel used to call me Apple Dumpling, and that's what I am. Anyway,

Arlan's always waited until whoever he had in mind came along. We all think it's you."

"Me?"

"Well, Arlan *needs* you. He wants to go places, see. He doesn't want to be tied down yet, with a baby and everything. You seem able to manage. I don't know how to explain it, Shelley, but you seem to be looking ahead more than most of the girls around here."

"Gosh, Janet, I've only known him for a couple of months. He doesn't have to make up his mind yet." Shelley poured herself more tea so she wouldn't have to look up.

"Arlan's going to move at all deliberate speed anyway," Janet said. "Don't worry about it."

"I'm not. I've got a lot of other things on my mind. Vernon of course. He's—" Shelley didn't finish, and Janet's face took on a solemn look.

"You've got Catherine, too," Janet said hesitantly. Shelley looked up. "She's been hanging around the tavern ever since your father got sick. Craig told me. Did you know that?"

Shelley didn't answer. It wasn't that she hadn't suspected, hadn't known, but hearing it was a shock.

"There's some kind of tough fellers there in Port Huyett, the ones that hang out at the Dragger. You ought to keep an eye on her, Shelley," Janet warned. "Catherine's kind of a handful for you, I bet."

"Catherine hasn't been in for two days. Is she all right?" Vernon asked. Shelley didn't like to see him lying there in the hospital bed, almost as if he'd given up to it, as if he were glad of its shelter and support. Afraid that she would upset him, Shelley answered yes to his question. But it was a lie.

That afternoon, for a change, Shelley found Catherine at home in front of the TV. She put her books down on the table.

"Were you in town today?" she asked, trying not to sound threatening. "Vernon was wondering why you hadn't come in."

Catherine turned around, breaking off from the TV, and for once looked Shelley straight in the eye.

"Vernon gave me strict orders to stay out of your life, Shelley," she said softly. "Would you like to stay out of mine?"

Chapter 9

THEIR OLD FORD WAS NOT PARKED IN ITS USUAL place, on the lee side of a rock pile. Shelley, en route from school and halfway past the Brocks', couldn't see it anywhere. Vernon wasn't due home for another few days; she'd just seen him at noon at the hospital. And Catherine, if she even knew how to drive, had no license. . . . Shelley broke into a run.

Half an hour later Catherine drove into the parking space, and the car shuddered to a halt. Shelley, waiting anxiously in the doorway, blurted out, "Catherine! You . . ."

Catherine swept past her. "I took the test, and I have my driver's license!" she exulted. She fished a card out of her purse and laid it reverently on the table.

"But—" Shelley said and, hearing the admonition in her voice, stopped short. Her objection had been so automatic, so full of Vernon questions. Who was going to pay for the gasoline a liberated Catherine would burn up? The car repair? Was she covered by Vernon's insurance? Was she even capable of driving? Since she was spending most of her days at the Dragger, had she started to drink? Who had taught her, or retaught her, to drive, and who had driven her in for the test?

Shelley saw Catherine's triumphant flush give way to anger.

"See?" she cried, tossing her head, "I told you so. You're just Vernon all over again."

"I suppose I am," Shelley answered in as controlled a voice as she could manage. "But money's going to be a problem."

"It's your problem," Catherine retorted. "You could at least have said 'That's neat' or *something* like that." She snatched the license from the table, dropped it back in her purse, and stalked off to her bedroom.

Shelley felt about a thousand years old. It would have been so easy to say "That's neat" and coped afterward, she thought. Why *hadn't* she said it?

Like a homing pigeon, Vernon came back from the hospital and made straight for his cubbyhole under the stair. It was where he wanted to be, he said; he wouldn't be any trouble. Shelley made him a cup of tea, sad to see how weak he was.

"I've sold the Ford," he informed her wearily. "The man will be coming tonight to pick it up." Shelley gasped.

"But, Vernon," she said in distress. "Catherine just got her driver's license!"

"The two of you can't afford a car," Vernon said. He laid his cup down in exhaustion. "She has no business out on the road anyhow." He closed his eyes, and the discussion was over.

Catherine, her eyes teary with rage, hissed at Shelley when she returned to the kitchen. "I presume you managed that to your satisfaction. You got it all settled, didn't you?"

"I've made a lot of mistakes," Shelley answered quietly. "But I didn't make that one." She thought for a minute and then turned impulsively to Catherine. "Why don't you try to get a job?" she asked. "It would give you your own money. I can manage with Vernon, I think."

"And stand for hours every day, packing fish in that fish plant?"

"Well, not that maybe," Shelley said, startled. The idea of Catherine in a fish plant was incongruous, to say the least.

"There isn't *anything* in Sentinel Head, and there isn't anything else in town but the fish plant," Catherine snapped. "That I can do anyway. And you know it. Anyhow," she added with a toss of her head, "I have my own ways, and let me remind you, it's none of your business."

That discussion was over, too. Even before Vernon died, Shelley Joyner wasn't doing very well. When she was all alone, what then?

The lobster season started on the last day of November, and the lobster traps, which had been piled in front of or beside the houses, disappeared like magic. So did the men, Arlan included. He came home early from school and was soon out on the boats, setting traps. Shelley had naively supposed that the men would be far out at sea, and Arlan had laughed heartily at her. The shores were lined with boats and would be in all possible weather until late spring.

"All traps have to be out of the water May 31," Arlan said, "but we won't lobster that long. We usually start to fish by April." On rough days, when the men didn't go out, there was gear to repair, traps to mend. Arlan was going to be busy for a long time.

The gray days of December engulfed them, swallowing up any remaining vestiges of color and seeming to lay flat the very contours of the land. In the Joyner household, the days stretched themselves out in increasing weariness. Catherine announced to Vernon that she was going to town when and if she wanted to, and Vernon let her go, though even in his weakness he had not really loosened his control of the household. He was still the seat of their government. Shelley had finally understood that her great management skills had been in small things, at Vernon's sufferance. But now he seemed no longer to care what Catherine did or didn't do, as if on his organization chart he had simply pushed an unsuccessful project to the nonprofit column.

He slept a great deal, apparently most of the day, reserving his remaining energy for Shelley's return from school. Then, in his seedy old bathrobe and growing smaller and smaller, he sat gently rocking in the kitchen. After Catherine got home, the TV droned away in the living room and Shelley, working around both parents, tried desperately to cram a lifetime with her father into the few weeks that the doctor had promised.

Word got around. People from the neighborhood dropped by to offer help, to bring food that might tempt Vernon into eating. Shelley would come home and find that someone had installed a new pump or wrapped pipes for the winter. The kids at school were really nice, and in spite of her heavy sadness, she found that she was making friends, new ones. Arlan sat with her every day on the bus, and no one bothered to tease them about it. She hated to leave home in the evenings, and Arlan began to bring his books to their kitchen.

"Finishing up, are you?" Vernon asked one night.

Arlan nodded. "In January. I should have graduated last June, but Dad needed me to help out with the lobstering last term. I'll be signing up for the Coast Guard after the lobstering this spring."

"I wish I could be around to see . . . what happens to everyone," Vernon said sadly, and no one had the heart to answer him.

It was almost as if he had stopped eating—the

amounts got so small; but somebody brought him some homemade bread and he enjoyed it.

"I don't know why this tastes so good," he apologized.

Shelley walked up to the Brocks' after supper. "Could you teach me to make bread?" she asked.

"Of course, dear," Dru said. "Phoebe's coming to spend the day with me tomorrow. It's Saturday. We'll all bake together."

"Who's Phoebe?" Shelley asked Arlan.

"Her sister," Arlan answered. "They're a lot alike. They even look like twins. Phoebe's the housekeeper for a resort hotel up at Spruce Point, and when the manager leaves for the winter, she takes over."

"Where's Spruce Point?" Shelley asked.

"Couple of hours toward Halifax. By car," Arlan said. "Longer by boat."

Arlan was collecting his gear for the next day's lobstering. It was going to be cold, and Shelley noted with relief and some pride that his fisherman's mittens were going along.

"Is your aunt's hotel a nice place?" Shelley asked.

"Gosh, yes. The owner runs a condo or something in the Caribbean during the winter months and comes up here for the season—June through September. He and Phoebe have worked together for years; he gives her a lot of responsibility. She knows the local people, of course, and she hires the staff. She lives right there on the grounds with Uncle Tom. They have a little house for themselves, and she keeps part of the lodge open for a few people who live there all year round."

Arlan stuffed his wet-weather gear into a duffel bag and hoisted it to his shoulder.

"You'll like Phoebe," he said, smiling. "You'll like her a lot. And she'll like you."

"So you're Shelley. Well!" Phoebe Crandall exclaimed. Dru set a teapot out on the table, and the three of them sat down to a chatty cup while the yeast proofed in its own warm bowl. Shelley thought of Arlan out in the trawler, pitching on a cold sea. The women's world, at least here, was a lot more pleasant. Then with a shock she realized that she *was* part of that women's world, as Arlan was part of the men's. There could be no doubt about it, for the conversation included her, and it was not scaled down to child size.

"How is your father today?" asked Dru, and when Shelley described Vernon's increasing weakness, neither of the women made any attempt to reassure her or to argue that Vernon would surely recover. They knew about loss from personal experience and from a heritage of family and neighborhood saga. They recounted this lore as naturally as they drank their tea.

. . . She said the farewell was as sweet as the courtship. . . . The last thing she said was, just make sure I look warm. . . . Everyone listens for the last

90

words, and sometimes they're downright ridiculous
. . . those hours of that terrible breathing. . . .

It was apparent that the morning was to be dedi-
cated to her education. Arlan, out in his boat with his
father and older brother, must in just this way have
learned the whole machinery of fishing. Shelley
guessed she was receiving instruction in the machinery of dying.

She enjoyed the bread making, every second of
it. Dru lugged a huge crockery mixing bowl from the
cupboard and set it on the table.

"I thought I could get along without a crock,
once," commented Phoebe. "Someone in the hotel
kitchen dropped mine. They're very dear, you know.
Well, I thought I could raise bread in stainless steel."

"Phoebe! In that cold kitchen!"

"Right! Oh, my dear, what a disaster! I *couldn't*
get the dough warm. Right there on the sea edge,
you know, and then I tried to warm it in the oven,
and I got the dough too hot and killed it off. . . ."

Dru turned the kneading over to Shelley, and
both sisters coached from the sidelines.

"She's got a way with bread," observed Phoebe,
nodding at her sister. Shelley had shaped the now
silky dough into a smooth ball and was putting it to
bed, as they said, in the warm, buttered crock. The
bread felt alive. She stroked its top rather as if it were
a pussycat sunning in a window.

"Dru, you always stroke the bread, too!" Phoebe
pointed out.

91

Shelley did like energetic Phoebe Crandall. Arlan was right, and she bet Phoebe was one fine manager. Phoebe was glad to have the management of the hotel when her husband was out fishing. She didn't have to think about him, what might be happening out there at sea, though things were better now for the fishermen, she admitted. The hotel was already closed for the winter, except for the few permanent guests and an occasional drop-in. The hotel overlooked the open ocean, and a person had to be hardy to live there through the storms, but the old girls who stayed on were indestructible, she said.

Throughout the morning, drinking tea, chatting, waiting for the bread to rise, they spent a lot of the time laughing at Phoebe's stories. Like Dru, she was plainly more practical than sentimental, and she was perfectly capable of poking fun at some of the hotel patrons, in a nice, earthy sort of way. She was taking on another court case in a few days, a kid involved in a motorcycle accident, about to be released from Orthopedic Hospital.

"Phoebe hires these young people for a few months and lets them sort of work through their problems. She's helped a lot of them," Dru said with an approving nod.

"They're my children," Phoebe explained.

"I'd like to manage a hotel," Shelley said slowly. "I'd like to learn how. I've always liked to get things done."

"Well, good," said Phoebe. "We'll work on that." The promise went right to Shelley's heart.

"Come and visit for a day," Phoebe suggested. "You might like to get a feel for the place."

"Why not?" Dru responded. "Arlan can drive her up. He could use a break about now. Axel sometimes forgets the boys have lives of their own."

It occurred to Shelley on the way home that she was actually happy. Happy! It was a sacrilege, under her present circumstances. She couldn't help it, though. She sniffed her loaf through its wrappings. The Brock family—Phoebe, Arlan, all of them—generated light, and like the sunshine of Dru's lemon pie on the Joyner's first night in Sentinel Head, their simply being up the road, a caring family, brightened the worst that this gray December could bring.

Chapter 10

SPRUCE POINT! ARLAN AND SHELLEY HAD BEEN driving for a good two hours, but now signs along the roadside began to advertise the ocean resort with its various attractions: golf was one of them.

"It's neat of Phoebe to ask us out!" Shelley exclaimed. "Arlan, do you play golf?" The truck jolted in surprise.

"*Golf!*" Arlan looked as amazed as if she'd inquired about his last visit to outer space. "Spruce Point is a different world," he commented. "Phoebe just manages the place; she doesn't live that kind of life."

"Well, I didn't think she did. I just think it's a miracle we're spending the day out here."

"I think it's a miracle Dad let me off for a whole Saturday in the middle of the lobstering," Arlan said grimly. "He must be off his rocker."

"He skippers his boat, all right, but Dru really runs your house. She thinks you need a good time now and then." Shelley grinned at the unexpected blue day outside the truck window. "What I'm grateful for is a better day for Vernon," she added. "For a change. He really wanted me to go."

"Things aren't easy for you," Arlan said soberly. "Let's celebrate. We'll pretend we're from New York and have a million dollars."

They turned off the highway, and after some winding seaward on increasingly narrow lanes and passing the golf course, now deserted, they came to the resort entrance. A curved drive led up to a rustic, but in Shelley's eyes, elegant hotel. In her first glance, Shelley took in the ocean, which the hotel overlooked, the pine woods surrounding the building, the cabins tucked into them, the inviting sidewalks leading to and from places, and gardens now empty, but she could imagine them splashy with asters, marigolds, and mums. Arlan drove his truck into an area below the driveway, where service vehicles of various sorts were congregated and where a row of motellike cottages appeared to house the resort workers, though most of the area looked closed up for the winter.

"Phoebe and Tom live down at the end house," Arlan commented. "We'll see if she's there. If not, we'll find her up at the lodge."

No one answered their knock, so they walked up to the main building and into the lobby. Through the windows of the dining room beyond, Shelley could see the uninterrupted ocean, the breakers rolling in to a long beach. A drawing room opened off the lobby, down a few steps, and it, too, looked out to sea. Arlan took her elbow, for she had frozen to the spot, absorbing it all, and he steered her to the reception desk. There a young girl, not a day older than Shelley, was gloriously employed with mailboxes, the switchboard, ledgers, file boxes, keys. Shelley's soul was instantly filled with longing.

Phoebe, summoned, came in from somewhere and greeted them with enthusiasm.

"We're not busy with guests," she said. "Just a few upstairs, and one honeymooning couple who insisted we open up a favorite cabin. Why don't you show Shelley around, Arlan? Be back in an hour, though. I've set you up for lunch in the dining room."

They were like kids in an amusement park, racing from the swimming pool—drained now of course, its machinery all collapsed into its insides—to the various sun porches, common room, bars, and game room. One of the cabins was open. A cart, stacked high with chemicals and cleaning tools, stood by the open door, and presently a young girl in uniform, Shelley's age again, emerged from the inside to collect her vacuum cleaner.

"Sure, come on in," she said. "See how the other half lives."

Shelley walked inside and stood in the center of the living room. She couldn't believe it—picture windows looked out to sea, and a patio door opened onto a balcony where you could sit and watch the surf forever if you wanted to. She thought the furnishings were the most elegant she'd ever imagined: the square, upholstered chairs; the angled sofas; the coffee table that fit in front of them, inviting a leisurely life; a breakfront whose apparent function was just to stand there and do nothing at all. Underneath, the carpet was soft enough to roll in. All this just for vacation. She walked into the bedroom, Arlan behind her.

The huge bed was open, rumpled, the pillows pushed together in the center, the blankets tossed about and lying half on the floor. Shelley took a hasty step backward, bumping into Arlan. It was too intimate. She might just as well have walked in on the lovers themselves, two lucky people romping in that enormous bed or perhaps lying happily side by side, each taking comfort in the nearness of the other. Her mind raced on, fiercely insisting on turning those two people into herself and Arlan, on moving one into the shelter of the other's arms, and beyond. . . .

Shelley pushed past Arlan, desperate for the cool outside. He followed her out to the porch.

"Gosh, Arlan," she gasped.

Arlan stood beside her, leaning against the cabin side and looking patiently out to sea. Shelley wondered how much he had guessed.

"I'd like to live like that someday, Shelley," he said seriously.

Shelley shook her head. "There's an awful lot of space between that and either of us."

"Someday," Arlan repeated. "I mean it." They

stood there for a little while, watching the breakers and listening to the combo of vacuum cleaner and breaking surf.

"I'd like to work here," Shelley said at last. "I really would."

"Making beds and things?" Arlan asked.

"Well, I do that at home already," Shelley pointed out. "It's doing it here that's different."

Arlan put his arm around her. "It's how Phoebe started out. And now she's in charge of even more than the housekeeping. You could do it, Shelley," he said. "Sure you could." He kissed her.

Phoebe put them at a table for two, by a window looking out over the long beach and the surf riding in on it. A number of guests were in the dining room, some rather tottery old ladies wrapped up in piles of sweaters, some people who had just stopped in for luncheon, and presumably the honeymooning couple so absorbed in each other that they might just as well have been eating in a cafe down the road. Neither Shelley nor Arlan had the faintest idea of what to do with the fancy goblets and piles of silverware. Phoebe, flying back and forth, teased them mercilessly about it. The waiter, a young kid from a neighboring town, got to giggling with them as he magnificently presented them with sandwiches stuck together with little flags and chowder in cups with two handles and two completely useless plates underneath.

"So much for the leisured class," Phoebe said bluntly, pulling up a chair and joining Shelley and Arlan at coffee. "Back to work. I'm short at the desk this afternoon, Shelley, and I need you. Arlan, Tom's not lobstering this year. He's tying up for the winter, and he could use a hand if you don't mind."

Phoebe showed Shelley the main functions of the desk, nothing very difficult. She left some envelopes to be stuffed, sealed, and stamped and some bills to be filed. The switchboard was already turned off for the winter, and calls were handled by a relatively simple system of buzzers.

"I'll be in my office," Phoebe explained. "Mostly all you need do is buzz. For the rest, you're on your own."

Shelley spent the afternoon in an ecstasy of small jobs. The desk was dusty and needed straightening, and she set about cleaning it up, throwing out a tired bouquet and replacing it with a potted plant sitting without function in one of the lobby windows. She thought things looked a lot better when she was through, and she wondered why the girl in the morning hadn't thought to clean up. She couldn't have been *that* busy! A few people came in from the outside: deliverymen, the postman, and a couple of people who just wanted to look around and eventually asked their way to the rest rooms. But they all stopped to chat for a few minutes. Phoebe had some telephone calls, and a man with a briefcase came in and asked to see her. Shelley, out of some instinct, politely inquired as to his name and business and relayed the information to Phoebe by phone. "Oh, I'll be right up," she said, laughing and, when she got to the desk, greeted the man as an old friend. "Glad to see you, Dennis. I'm into restocking, and I was about to call you."

"Giving the place an uplift, I see." The man waved his hand toward the reception area, and Phoebe, glancing toward the desk, smiled. "Permanent, I trust," the man added. Shelley felt herself blushing. She'd assumed the uplift meant the desk.

"Thank you for cleaning up, Shelley," Phoebe said quietly and smiled again as she went off down the hall with the salesman.

It hadn't hurt, the compliment, though Shelley honestly couldn't see why he'd made it. She wasn't even dressed up, just jeans and a T-shirt—and she couldn't see what the uplift was all about.

"You had a good time today, didn't you, Shelley?" Arlan asked as they started home in the truck later that afternoon. "Your cheeks have been bright red all day, and I thought your eyes were just going to pop out."

"I must have looked enchanting."

"You did," Arlan said gravely.

Shelley looked across at him. He was watching the road as he drove, but he seemed not to be seeing it. His face, framed by his windblown hair, looked worried, a little puckered when he frowned. He was really cute, she thought all over again, especially when something was on his mind as it was now, and his feelings were showing all over his features.

"It's easy to envy Janet and Craig," Arlan said. Shelley jumped and looked at him suspiciously. She hadn't said one word! Not even to Janet. "It seems . . . so easy, like," Arlan continued, struggling for words. "They seem to have everything, getting married and all."

"Well, it's really nice for them. Janet's so much in love," Shelley ventured. "She's awfully happy." She could suddenly picture Janet and Craig in that bed, really happy, and the same longing engulfed her again.

"They could wait maybe," Arlan said cautiously. "If they have a baby right away, Craig won't ever get out of fishing. He'll be stuck with it, just like Dad and Clyde. He'll . . ."

"Arlan," Shelley said, putting her hand on his arm, "are you talking about Craig and Janet, or are you talking about Arlan Brock?"

"Arlan Brock," answered Arlan. "And also about Shelley Joyner."

"Well, if you're talking about Shelley Joyner," continued Shelley, "she has a lot of responsibilities right now, Vernon and all, plus not wanting to end up like Catherine. And if you're talking about Arlan Brock, he's going into the Coast Guard, and I mean it."

Arlan's worried face smoothed out, and then it edged around into his puckish grin.

"Shelley," he said, "the minute I can get around this damn oil truck ahead of me, I'm going to kiss you."

He did, but the longing she'd felt all day remained. It was sweet, but it worried her. It was all right to fall in love, because that was what she was doing, but no one had told her that she would ache all over.

Phoebe Crandall

Phoebe continued to stand in the lodge doorway, watching Arlan and Shelley take off down the road. Arlan was her favorite nephew; he'd been a naturally charming, albeit stubborn, baby and youngster, and she thought he hadn't changed much. She liked this Shelley. She agreed with Dru that Arlan had made up his mind from the start. Of course, Shelley was an outsider, something new. And she was a no-nonsense girl, self-directed, what Arlan was looking for. She was kind and conscientious as well. Perhaps too much of the latter, Phoebe thought. She'd push herself pretty hard. You could set standards for yourself that were too high for this hard old world and stumble badly.

And Shelley had a rough row to hoe. Phoebe agreed with Dru about that. The father could not last much longer, and, obviously, the mother was a handful. Shelley, Dru said, was as stubborn as Arlan when it came to accepting help. Both of them had it to learn: you can't go it alone forever.

Phoebe smiled to herself. She liked young people and was looking forward to seeing what she could do with the motorcycle case. She'd have to get in touch with Sarah Luddington in Sentinel

Head, get his records transferred to the local high school.

Phoebe turned away from the door. She wished Arlan and Shelley well. She felt a little protective of the girl, possessive even, because of Arlan. She couldn't help envying Dru a little.

Sarah Luddington

In a moment of respite from student problems, Sarah turned from her desk and looked out her window, seaward. Winter had arrived, no mistake, the long, dark days. Things happened in the gray winter months, a lot of stress and tragedy.

Phoebe Crandall had telephoned, and Sarah had enjoyed talking to her. She was relieved that Michael would be coming to her. The boy was crushed in more than body. It would be a long time before he worked through the death of his friend, and his family was already under too much stress to give him much help. She wondered why these families, hardly able to get by, seemed to end up with motorcycles. And accidents.

Phoebe had talked a little about Shelley Joyner. There was another potential tragedy. Shelley was an appealing girl. Able. Arlan Brock was a lucky chap, and she hoped he knew it. That kind of girl didn't turn up often.

It was a lot for a young person to handle, the father dying, the mother somewhat of a problem and not likely to fit into the community. Sarah had heard the mother was hanging around the Dragger daytimes. She sighed. Shelley was obviously happy here, back in the land of her ancestors, as it were. One could only hope that if the mother tried to yank Shelley up after the father passed away, her roots would be dug in too deep to let go.

Chapter 11

THERE WAS NO STOPPING THE TRUE WINTER WHEN it came, though, because of their closeness to the water, it brought no snow, only roaring seas, wind, and a blackness on the land. To Shelley it presaged the end of everything.

She didn't see very much of Arlan. He slipped into the Joyner house when he could, to lend a hand, though there wasn't much he could do. When Vernon was asleep, Shelley let the wind push her up the road to the Brocks', and coming home, she braced herself against it, just as she braced herself for the grim facts within. Catherine, not relishing the cold walk out to the bus stop, and perhaps out of decency to Vernon as well, stopped going to town unless Dru was able to take her. Catherine listened endlessly to TV, Shelley listened to Vernon's labored breathing and to the sea's continual moan, and they waited.

"Shouldn't we call Billy?" Shelley asked one evening. "Wouldn't he want to know?"

"What could *he* do?" Catherine answered. "He hated Vernon anyway. He got out as soon as he could."

Shelley, annoyed, shrugged and let it go.

The Saturday after the trip to Phoebe's Dru had taken Catherine into town with her, and Vernon called to Shelley.

"There's a billfold in the dresser," he said. Shelley opened the drawer and brought out an old leather wallet. She'd never seen it before.

"There's four hundred dollars in there. Keep it hidden somewhere in case you need it, Shelley. Don't let Catherine have it—she'll spend it in an afternoon."

"Vernon . . ." There was so much to ask him.

"The lawyer will see to things," he said wearily. "Mr. Barrett, I think that was his name. I've arranged to have my retirement check go directly to his office, and after the first of the month, you'll have to pick it up there. Don't let Catherine get her hands on it, Shelley. I warn you. I've left the house in trust to you, too, Shelley. This will give the two of you a roof over your heads, and she won't be able to sell it away from you on some fool whim or another. She can't leave without resources, no job or anything."

"I hope you're right," Shelley said soberly. "You never know with Catherine."

"She can't get her hands on either the house or my retirement, Shelley," Vernon insisted.

104

"Does she know you've done all this?" Shelley asked. Vernon nodded.

"She's been having tantrums all week, when you weren't here. She's caught, but it's her fault. She had her chance, long ago. Do what you can for her, Shelley. But remember I told you there are limits. I brought you home. It was the right thing to do. And I want you to stay here."

The next week Vernon slipped in and out of awareness. One afternoon Shelley happened on the *Messiah* as she switched stations on the radio. She automatically never stopped at the classical music station, so she was unprepared when Vernon asked to listen to it. She wasn't sure how much he actually heard, but once he laughed.

" 'Great was the company of the preachers.' I can just see them lined up there in a row," he murmured.

Shelley found most of the music incomprehensible, not to say boring, but once in a while either the words or the melody caught her attention. At one point Catherine wandered into Vernon's room and sat down. She stayed there quietly, listening for a while and then, restless, got up and returned to her place by the TV, out of sight in the sitting room.

"Take care of her, Shelley," Vernon whispered. And then, tremulously, "Promise me you will." He began to cry, the tears rolling helplessly down his cheeks and into the pillow.

"Of course I will, Vernon," Shelley answered. "I'll do all I can. Truly." There was a limit to what anyone could do for Catherine; he'd said so. But Shelley made a promise wholeheartedly. He dropped off, the tears still wet on his cheeks.

Shelley fled to her room. Vernon was forty-three. She'd always thought of him as old, but now she knew how terribly young he really was, hardly more than halfway through his life, so many projects incomplete. She herself, for instance. It was intolerable that he'd never know what happened to her, never complete the fatherhood she'd been so late to recognize. In his self-effacing life, he'd missed so much. He'd never even gotten out to the Head. All her life she'd be thinking of places he'd never seen that she would have liked to show him.

Vernon had spent his life—she'd finally understood this—not in ridiculous grubbing, as Catherine complained, but in selfless and patient work, reaping almost nothing for himself. If Catherine had been childish in her constant reaching for more, his own daughter had been unthinking in her acceptance of what harvest he was able to offer her. Shelley started to cry, and kneeling at the window, hoping perhaps to find some answer to her sorrow in the reaches of the sea, she sobbed for a long time, almost in relief.

With as little fuss as he had made in life, Vernon died early the next morning, before dawn. Shelley knew he was gone because it was so terribly quiet when she went into his bedroom.

As if in compensation for or even to counteract the bleakness of December, Sentinel Head had decked itself in an extravagance of Christmas lights and decoration. On the grayest of days and in the heart of this tinseled illumination, a group of neighbors, Old Jaimie, Janet, Vernon's solicitor from town, and unexpectedly a young nurse from the hospital who said Vernon had been kind to her gathered at the grave site. Shelley, seeing the open grave, could not imagine how the Brock men could ever have dug so far into the cold, stony soil. Thus it was, in a remote community, surrounded by fishermen and their families, and within sound of the moaning sea, that Vernon's life was officially to end.

As the minister, a local man suggested by the Brocks, droned on in an overlong prayer, Shelley's attention was caught by a movement from Catherine. The wind had disarranged her hair. With her eyes fixed on the horizon and far beyond the present scene before her, she lifted both arms and worked the stray lock back into place. It was an incongruous gesture, at odds with the respectful dignity of the group around the grave, and Shelley cringed. The gray world of sky, sea, and earth had taken Vernon back into its own, and she hadn't been able to do one single thing to stop it. How was she to "take care of" Catherine, as she had promised? She didn't know how. She didn't even know how she was going to take care of herself. She looked over the heads of the group to the gray sea, but she found no answer there.

Arlan was standing behind her, and he gently put his arms around her and drew her close in. It was the only answer she had.

Chapter 12

THE LONELY CHRISTMAS, THOUGH THE BROCKS AND the other neighbors did their best to cheer it, was finally over, and January bore in, with icy cold from the northwest and a startlingly beautiful snowfall. January turned out to be not so dismal, weatherwise, as December had been. The sun shone often in the brief hours of daylight, and Shelley found she was enduring. It wasn't that she didn't miss Vernon, because she did, but the worst so far as he was concerned was over, and the rest simply had to be faced.

The new school term had started. The school bus seemed very empty. Arlan was through with school and out on the lobster boat full time. Catherine picked up her life, spending her days in town.

"What do they do there all day?" Shelley asked Janet.

"Oh, I don't know. Craig says they show up middle of the morning, just cackling and jawing away. It's so noisy in there anyhow, with those pool tables and the balls banging away and the TV on or the jukebox going full tilt. They sit there and drink coffee, and then at lunch they get going on the beer."

"So I gather," Shelley commented. "The fumes nearly knock me over in the afternoon." It wasn't much of a surprise. Catherine was just repeating the pattern from No-Hope and the days of Mary Ann.

Maybe it was disturbing, Shelley thought, because she had no idea who Catherine's friends were, and Catherine wasn't exactly communicative. She appeared to be thriving, though. Maybe it was the long walk out to the bus or because she wasn't so lonely anymore. She looked better, younger, than she had for a long time. On rough days someone drove her home from town; who it was, Shelley had no idea and she didn't ask. Catherine came home in the evenings, conversed casually about the weather, or commented on small details of local gossip that she had picked up at the Dragger. Occasionally she asked, without much interest, about Shelley's school. But it was obvious Shelley was not invited into her life.

Shelley had Vernon's wallet, for emergencies, he'd said, but she had made up her mind to use it for something else. Vernon had lived an anonymous life, but there was a heroism to it if you didn't aim too high. He'd cared for his family, he'd been courageous in transplanting them to an unknown community, he'd taken a gamble, a dangerous one, and he'd been really brave in the way he faced death. His heroism deserved a tribute. He may have been anonymous in life, but he wasn't going to be completely anonymous in death.

Early in January she visited the Shore Monument Company in town. A carved headstone was clearly beyond her means, and she settled, in cash, for a simple stone engraved with Vernon's name and span of life. She didn't tell Catherine what she had done. Why should she?

Two weeks later, early on a Saturday morning, the headstone was delivered. Catherine was still asleep, and Shelley chose not to awaken her. She drove out to the cemetery with the truck driver to see that the headstone was properly placed, but a cruel wind from the sea prevented her from lingering for more than a minute or two. That and a sudden, horrible, growing anger against Vernon. How had he expected her to cope with Catherine? The anger, the mere thought of it, was so devastating, so indecent, that she stamped it down, refusing ever, she assured herself, to look it in the face again. It didn't stop the anger.

She had other worries as well. Vernon's January pension check had not arrived. Shelley had called at the solicitor's office twice, but the secretary who had been assigned to her affairs looked surprised, riffled papers, and said without much interest, "No dear, it hasn't come yet. All this red tape, of course."

The secretary may not have been concerned, but Shelley was. The food brought in when Vernon died—Shelley had packaged and frozen it—was running low, and would soon be gone, and it wouldn't be long before Catherine would be demanding more bus and lunch money.

By the third week of January, they were almost out of food. Catherine was eating at the tavern, but Shelley, who brown-bagged it to school to save lunch money, was down to mostly bread. She refused to consider Vernon's emergency fund, what was left of it, after paying for the stone. This was not an emergency, she told herself; it was an incident, a mere adjustment. She'd rough it out.

Bread was supposed to be the staff of life, but she wasn't finding it all that sustaining, and she was, in fact, hungry. She walked over to the attorney's office at noon. The monthly check was still not there. Exasperated, desperate, she confronted the secretary.

"Look!" She heard herself yelling. "Maybe it doesn't worry you, but we need that money. *Where is it?*"

The secretary picked up the phone and dialed. The check had been mailed the first of the month, not to the lawyer, but to the Joyners' home address. So that was it! Catherine.

"We'll see that you get the next one through this office," the secretary said apologetically. "It's due in a couple of days. Can you manage?"

"Yes," Shelley snapped, stalking out. Like Vernon, she wasn't going to ask for quarter, and with the eyes of all the people in the office on her, she wasn't going to make the scene any worse.

But when Catherine came home that afternoon with two complete new outfits, shoes, handbags, everything, and bland defiance about them, Shelley hit the ceiling.

"You stole Vernon's check!" she shouted. "What am I supposed to do about food and things?"

"You seem to have plenty of money for tombstones," Catherine said coldly. "I heard about that down at the Dragger, not from you, by the way. Vernon gave you the car money, I gather. Well, you have your money, and I have mine." She picked up her packages and walked off to her bedroom.

The next morning Shelley was genuinely hungry. Tea and one slice of bread hardly dented her hunger. She thought of the wallet, hidden under the eaves upstairs. It was dumb, maybe, but she had made up her mind. She wouldn't touch one single nickel of the money. By noon she was ravenous. She couldn't believe how hungry you could get in a single morning. She walked out on the beach while the others ate, but on her way back into the building, she passed by the garbage cans outside the lunch room. An uneaten sandwich lay on top of the other stuff, and Shelley snitched it. Hoping no one had seen her, she bolted into the girls' room and wolfed the sandwich down.

A short time later she was summoned to the principal's office. Her heart sank, but she had to obey, and she stalked in through the door, ready for battle.

"What did you have for breakfast, Shelley?" Mrs. Luddington asked, looking up.

"Bread and tea," she answered shortly.

"And what did you have for supper last night?" Mrs. Luddington persisted.

"I'm all right, really," Shelley said desperately. "My father's check didn't come—where it was supposed to—but another one's due tomorrow."

Mrs. Luddington laid a ticket on the desk. "Go down to the cafeteria and get some dinner," she said quietly. It was charity, and Vernon would have died with embarrassment. Shelley put her hands behind her back.

Mrs. Luddington turned toward the window. "This is a fishing community, Shelley," she said.

"Look out there." Shelley looked at the beach, where she'd been standing in plain view during the lunch hour, and then out to the open sea.

"If you were in trouble out there, at sea, in a boat, do you think this town, the people in it, would just stand on the beach and *watch*?" Mrs. Luddington asked. "We'd send a boat out after you, wouldn't we? Now take the ticket and go and get your dinner."

That night there was a brief pounding on the back door. It was Axel. His honest face was flushed to his light hair; his blue eyes snapped. He was furious, and Shelley swallowed nervously.

"I ran into Sarah Luddington this afternoon, and I want to talk to your mother," he said gruffly. "You're to go down to the house, Shelley. Dru's fixing your supper."

Shelley put on her coat, glancing furtively at Catherine, who looked like a small child caught in sin. When Shelley let herself into the Brock kitchen, she found both Arlan and Dru all upset.

"Shelley, how *could* you go hungry like that!" Dru cried, and her eyes filled with tears. "What do you think we're here for?" Arlan looked too stricken to speak. He plied her with food, though she tried to explain that she'd had her dinner and wasn't exactly dying. She wondered what Axel was saying to Catherine.

It was Shelley's turn—and Arlan's—when Axel got back.

"Arlan, I thought you were looking after her.

For God's sake, you could at least have taken her a lobster!" Axel shouted. "Just because we weren't fishing. . . ."

"She said she didn't like lobsters," Arlan said miserably. Axel continued to shout.

"Well, we have a whole freezer full of fish, don't we? What's the matter with you, anyhow?"

"I'm sorry. It was really dumb of me, Axel," Shelley said. And it had been. She'd had money, after all. And now she'd gotten everyone in trouble. She was worried to death about Catherine. She was still furious at her, but having Axel light into her could be a real problem, and she was responsible for it. She started to put on her coat.

"That coat isn't warm enough for out here," Axel growled, feeling its weight. "Dru, where's that old pea jacket of Arlan's?"

"It's still in my closet," Arlan said. "I'll get it." He brought it from his room, put it on her, and hugged her besides.

"Things will work out. Don't give up, Shelley. Hang in there," he whispered to her. Shelley went home, warm all over.

Catherine was waiting for her. Her color was high, and her eyes bright and excited. There was a small stack of bills in the center of the table.

"There's the rest of the money," she said, as if she were repeating a lesson at school. "It was really decent of you to have that stone made for Vernon, Shelley."

Shelley looked at her in sudden comprehension

and saw the child, the headstrong, spoiled, indulged child, standing before her, scolded and chastened.

"He really bawled me out," Catherine said in longing. "Just the way Papa used to when I did something wrong. Axel said he was disappointed in me. Axel's some kind of man, isn't he, Shelley?"

Chapter 13

WHEN SHELLEY GOT HOME FROM SCHOOL THE NEXT day, Catherine was at home. Two gallons of paint sat on the table along with miscellaneous sacks and bags.

"I've been waiting for you, Shelley," Catherine said eagerly. Then she spoke rapidly, as if someone had pushed a button on some memorized bit she had been forced into learning for a school program. "I've been thinking about what Axel said," she recited. "He told me I wasn't doing very well as a parent. He told me they can turn you in for not taking care of your kids, even when they're as old as you are." She paused. Correct so far? she seemed to be asking.

Shelley nodded, wary, and waited to see where Catherine was headed.

"Well, I returned a lot of the clothes I bought," Catherine explained, "and I got this paint instead. I've decided to paint your bedroom."

* * *

Shelley wanted it too much. Not just the bed-room, though she couldn't help being excited by the prospect of a pretty one, but the first prolonged display of maternal care and interest she could remember.

The room was to be a surprise, and Catherine giggled as she told Shelley the upstairs was off limits. Shelley didn't dare offer to help. When she came home after school and found Catherine splotched with paint, even her hair sprayed with it, and saw her flop with fatigue into her chair in the kitchen, it was all Shelley could do—in fact it was the hardest work she'd *ever* done—not to offer to take over and do it for her.

For several days Catherine was dotted with white, but one evening she turned blue. "Vernon would have a fit over this," she observed.

"Why?" Shelley asked, dying of curiosity.

"Your father was such a nuts-and-bolts man. He never did anything in his life but grub. It wouldn't have occurred to him to paint the ceiling blue." Ceiling! Blue! It wouldn't have occurred to me either, Shelley thought with excitement.

"I got the idea out of a magazine at the beauty parlor," Catherine explained. "It's just perfect. I can hardly wait till you see it."

When Shelley at last saw Catherine's blue-and-white room, she couldn't believe it. The last couple of weeks had been happy, filled with a sense of achievement, but now her cup of happiness over-flowed. The blue ceiling invited in the sky. The furniture, white, even the old desk! And frilly priscillas at the window! A bedspread! a little rag rug beside her bed!

"I got everything at the next-to-new place," Catherine said in satisfaction.

"Mother, it's just beautiful," Shelley said at last and from the heart. But Catherine continued to admire her handiwork, as happy as a youngster home from school, a gift of school craft clutched in her fist. If she heard Shelley call her "Mother," and with feeling, she chose not to respond.

"Well, I guess it ought to satisfy Axel," she said calmly.

So *Axel* had momentarily made her toe the mark, pushed her into line with paternal authority, Shelley thought sadly. Axel was clearly out of her reach, as parent, husband, "some kind of man," whatever. Catherine's exercise had neither deepened her affection for Shelley nor assured in any way a further accommodation of Catherine to Sentinel Head. She'd done it for Axel; that was all. She hoped he'd pat her on the head, probably, tell her what a good girl she was.

So what *was* the use of trying, over and over and over? Why keep hoping, even? Well, she'd promised Vernon. Perhaps somehow, somewhere down the line . . .

"Thanks, anyway, Catherine," Shelley said steadily. "I really mean it."

As February wore on into March, Shelley wondered that there were any lobsters left in the ocean.

Arlan showed up, chapped and raw about the face and hands, only when foul weather pushed even the bravest of boats back to shore. The year's money was made in lobsters, not fish, and Arlan, no more than the other men, was spared the hard work and long hours.

In one stiff blow during the month, when it was too rough for the boats, Arlan drove Shelley to a nearby harbour town. He clearly had some mission in mind, for he raced the truck down the highway, muttering only that he hoped "she" was still there. They lumbered past the oil refinery and odoriferous fish plant at the lower end of the wharf and came into full view of a Coast Guard cutter, moored at the dock's end. RESCUE, Shelley read, and below it, SAUVETAGE. The cutter rocked casually in the angry sea, and Shelley could only think how beautiful she would look to a ship in trouble, that red, white, and piercing orange vessel, standing off some wreck or fire or sinking, way out at sea.

"I want her so much my face aches," Arlan said, and Shelley felt a throb of sadness for him, his weather-battered face was so full of longing. They got out of the truck, into a howling gale, but Arlan seemed hardly to notice it. He piloted her around, showing off the cutter as if he owned it, pointing out the special features.

"This one launches copters," Arlan said, studying a tremendous apparatus on the stern of the ship. Shelley in her turn was studying the lifeboats and the seamen, leaning against the cabins in the lee of the wind or hanging companionably over the rail, chatting to one another. Suddenly a garbled order blared out from the P.A. system, and the men jumped into action, disappearing on the run into various openings and holes in the ship.

"Won't you hate being told what to do all the time?" Shelley asked Arlan as the wind pushed them back into the truck. Arlan shook his head.

"Someone has to give orders," he said mildly. "Dad keeps telling me to bend my head, and he's right. If you're going to learn anything, you have to put up with it. I'm going to sign up soon as I can. Craig's going to take my place with Dad, but we have to wait for him to get married and settled in. Hey, Shelley," he said, grinning. "Let's call Janet and see if the four of us can go out somewhere this evening. I'm ready for a little fun. This has been one long winter."

"When does the lobstering end?" Shelley asked. "If ever."

"The season isn't officially over till the end of May, but almost no one goes on that long. Lobsters get scarce, and the early fishing is usually pretty good. We're kind of winding up now." He stretched, like a bear waking up from a long sleep. Then he turned the key in the ignition, and the truck responded with its usual clattery shaking.

The winter *had* gone on forever. Catherine, once the bedroom was painted and the obligation to Axel taken care of, had returned to the Dragger, daytimes, evenings as well. Even though Shelley had made lots of friends in the little houses up and down Sentinel Head, with Arlan virtually out of her life because of the lobstering, the evenings had been some tedious. She was more than ready for a little fun, had been for a while.

There wasn't a lot for teenagers to do in the little fishing villages, dead of winter or, for that matter, anytime. Drive to another town. Eat. Cruise around. Park somewhere. The latter activity was obviously foremost in Catherine's mind.

"Oh, come on," Shelley said impatiently, getting into her jacket and breaking into Catherine's carping. She could be so annoying, like a persistent nipping insect.

"Well, I don't think it's very nice of you to go off and leave me here alone," Catherine finished up. Shelley turned and stared at her. She couldn't believe Catherine. Who did she think had been sitting at home alone for the last month?

"There's nothing to do around here anyway," Catherine complained.

If there wasn't a lot for teenagers to do, there wasn't a lot outside the home for adults in either Sentinel Head or Port Huyett. Shelley had to admit that. Most of the social life centered around family groups, and you had to belong to them. That left the tavern, and nobody could say Catherine wasn't making good use of it. Who it was who was bringing her home late evenings, Shelley had no idea.

"I don't fit here," Catherine pointed out.

"You haven't made enough effort to break in," Shelley said quietly. "I know it's not easy. I've been wondering if there weren't some things you could do to meet more of the women around here. They all seem to keep busy."

"All they do is cook," Catherine groaned. "That's all they think about. Or they sit there and crochet, and I hate that stuff. They all belong to churches, and we've never been into that. I hear them talking at the beauty parlor, and there isn't *anything* around here that I fit into. You're all wrapped up in Arlan, so *you* don't have to worry."

"Look, Catherine," Shelley said, hoping to deflect her, "Janet's getting married in three weeks, and . . ."

"Yes, and I suppose next *you'll* be deciding you've had enough of me, and you'll take off with Arlan, and then what am I supposed to do?" Catherine's voice rose, close to hysteria.

"Janet's invited both of us to the wedding," Shelley continued, refusing to hear Catherine's outburst. "You haven't had much chance to know anyone around here except the Brocks. Because of Vernon, I mean. At the wedding . . ."

"I wish we'd never heard of these damn Brocks," Catherine yelled. "I *told* you not to get mixed up with Arlan! And I'm not going to any wedding either!"

"Sure you are, Catherine," Arlan said, knocking briefly and then coming through the kitchen door. He walked over to Catherine and put his arm around her. "Sure you're going to the wedding," he said easily. "First to Janet's, and a *long* time later, to ours. If it's OK with Shelley, of course," he said, laughing. "Put on your things, Catherine. Mum and Dad are driving up the way a bit. Mum's going to look for a fancy wedding present for Janet, and she needs your help. We figured we could all go together on it." Arlan hurried Catherine on with a little pat to her rear, a gesture he'd never used with her, Shelley noted. And had better not.

"Thanks, Arlan," Shelley said in rather a wobbly voice.

"I figured you might need some help," he said and grinned down at her. "We've got to keep her as happy as we can," he added. "I just reminded Dad I'd told him once that whatever I brought home I intended to keep. Well, Shelley, I intend to keep you, and I don't want Catherine in the way."

"She's already in the way, Arlan," Shelley said soberly. "I just hope not dangerously."

"She can't come between us," Arlan pointed out, and taking Shelley in his arms, held her close. "There isn't room."

Old Jaimie

Jaimie had not meant to become too involved with the Joyners. He'd established their identity, he'd talked to the girl about her grandfather and helped her out with the windows, he'd paid a duty call to Vernon and attended his funeral. He'd noted, with pleasure, that Arlan Brock seemed to be serious about the girl. Beyond that, and now that Vernon had passed away, he did not choose to go. He didn't want anything to do with the mother, for one thing. He didn't like her much. The woman didn't fit in up here: Jaimie had no time for the tavern regulars, men or women.

He worried about the girl. Outspoken she was, all right, direct and to the point, and when folks did her a favor, she paid a visit afterward, bearing gifts of bread that she had baked herself. He'd heard all that. One miserable evening she'd walked out on the Head and presented him with a loaf. Then she'd given him a hand with the chores. She didn't do it every night; he would have hated that, the obligation. But in spite of himself, his spirits lifted when he saw her bearing down on the farmhouse, and he appreciated her young strength. He'd drive her back to her house in the truck.

"Well, good-bye for now," she'd say cheerfully, with promise of more visits. They rarely talked. She respected his preferred silence.

No, he hadn't meant to become involved, even that far. Yet he woke up in the middle of the night, horrified at the thought that the mother might pull up roots and take Shelley away. He couldn't get back to sleep, and he was furious with himself.

Next day he made himself go to the Dragger, where he ordered an unaccustomed beer. Roy Manning, a swaggering roughneck, Jaimie thought, was back in town from Florida, visiting his folks. Jaimie watched the noisy table of regulars with a sardonic eye. Shelley's mother making time with Roy Manning. Well, they were two of a kind. He snorted, pushed back his unfinished beer, and limped out of the place.

Chapter 14

IT WAS AN EARLY SPRING, EVERYONE SAID. TOO
early. April . . . and they'd shake their heads. Shelley
didn't care. March was finally behind them. Those
who had taken off to avoid it were back now, like the
returning birds, and even if it was too early, the feeling of newness was everywhere.

The outdoors was irresistible, and Shelley and
Arlan began to visit the various beaches and hidden
points, much as Catherine and Vernon had done
those long months ago. Without apology, Shelley and
Arlan walked out on the Head in the evenings and
dropped around to visit Old Jaimie. It was all they
did, though, walk and sit in perfect contentment together on the rocks. Shelley was happier than she'd
ever been and also more miserable. She thought
Arlan was feeling the pressure, too, as if the spring
with its persistent force were pushing them faster
than they were prepared to go.

Craig and Janet had picked a Sunday afternoon
for their wedding day, a time after the lobsters and
before the new fishing season; but spring had gently
wrapped itself around the date, a wedding present.

Catherine was decked out second only to the
bride, Shelley thought in amusement. The dent in
their budget was little enough to pay for peace and

contentment, and Catherine did look pretty. Shelley prayed that all would go well. She rather gingerly put on the flimsy sandals she'd bought for the occasion and thought longingly of Catherine's arched and slender foot. She wondered, as she often did, why Arlan had chosen her, when he could have had almost anyone else. She took a last look in the bathroom mirror. She looked even more like a figurehead than she did last summer when she came here, because her cheeks were red from the sea air, her hair blonder and heavier, and her new dress brought out even more the painted blue of her eyes. What a horrible square chin she had, she thought. She must look really stubborn when she got mad. Poor Arlan! She sighed.

Janet had chosen to be married at home, and the ingathering of neighborhood and family was like a flower arrangement in itself. Shelley hadn't seen the men dressed up like this before, and she wondered what Catherine might be thinking. She hadn't realized how many of the families she herself had come to know. Most people there greeted her with warmth and affection. If they looked at Catherine a little diffidently, Shelley preferred not to see it.

Shelley had always liked Craig, a genial, an absolute Mr. Right for Janet. He detached himself from his family, where they were sort of grouped in one corner, and came over to say hello to her and to Catherine, whom he had not met.

"Sure is nice you folks could come," he said warmly. "Let me introduce you around, Mrs. Joyner. I don't know how many of these people you've met."

"None of them," Catherine replied ungraciously, and Shelley groaned. Craig winked at her, and she made an effort to smile back. No matter how much she might wish to ignore the fact, it was plain that *she* was accepted, a part of the community, but Catherine was there merely on polite sufferance. Catherine's hanging out at the Dragger was known; it wouldn't have gone down well, with the women particularly. Shelley wasn't sure about the men. Most of them dropped by the Dragger from time to time for a couple of beers with the chaps, and they couldn't have helped seeing Catherine. Nevertheless, Catherine appeared not to know them personally. It occurred to Shelley that Catherine's group, whoever they were, were not represented at this gathering at all.

Very soon Shelley was split off from Catherine by laughing young people, and then Arlan joined the group. Though Shelley kept an eye on Catherine, she couldn't really get back to her. It wasn't, however, until she saw Janet's granny-mum take her under her wings that she relaxed and set in to enjoy herself.

Janet now appeared, lovely, Shelley thought, from a bedroom. The crowd hushed, and the ceremony began. As she had at Vernon's funeral, Shelley felt Arlan standing behind her, and he put his arms around her, in possession this time, not comfort. In the gaiety following the ceremony, she and Arlan got well teased as the next couple out, and Shelley had to be pleased at Axel's unabashed grin, at Dru's flashing smile. Catherine was either not included in the banter, or she refused to join in. Her stony face would have scared anyone off, Shelley thought, and it wasn't until dear Granny-mum again made some remark to her that Catherine appeared to thaw at all. There were refreshments, the cutting of the cake, the tossing of the bouquet.

"Hey, Shelley!" Janet called, and Shelley dived for it. The couple left in a shower of rice, and the wedding was over. Shelley got ready to leave. She was taking away with her more than Janet's bouquet, though, or her joy in Janet's happiness. She'd understood so much. The marriage rite had been overlaid by the merriment and comfort of families that had attended countless such weddings together in familiar surroundings. The ebb and flow of generations were as much a part of the community memory as the ceremony itself, the affection coming from a long way back to enhance the new couple and the promise of family to come.

Shelley felt a part of the whole thing, almost as if she were the bride. She looked for Catherine, but Catherine had already left and gone back to the house alone.

"Well, *you* sure have everything," Catherine threw at Shelley. They had taken off their finery and were back to basics. "All your friends and everything. Arlan. I wish I could say the same for me." She stood in front of a little mirror she'd hung as a checkpoint in the kitchen.

Shelley had her own checkpoints, a thermometer, the tide charts, and outside the window a little wind gauge she had devised. She was peering at it now in concern, and although she heard Catherine and correctly gauged the weather, both inside and out, she didn't answer, holding off the serious realities until the last moment.

"All that damn paint for your bedroom. My hair's a mess," Catherine moaned. "Ever since I did that painting, I can't do anything with it. I had to wash it almost every day, and now it's all dried out."

"The wind's shifted," Shelley commented, still avoiding the issue. "It seems to be veering to the east."

"So what?" Catherine retorted, furiously patting and shaping at her hair.

"But that means a storm."

"Well, let it storm!" Catherine snapped. "As if that's anything new around here. Well, have we enough money left so I can have my hair done or not? I'm going into town tomorrow."

Shelley counted out the money and gave it to her. She sighed. Everything in her own game of chance had turned up roses, but Catherine was still over in the corner, recklessly—desperately—throwing quarters into the slot. What *did* the threat of a storm matter to her? If the storm tore everything in Sentinel Head to splinters, would she care?

"You and Vernon weren't very happy together," Shelley ventured at last. "Was it always that way?"

Catherine sat down at the table. She looked pretty beat, and Shelley was sorry she'd asked. But as Catherine began to talk, her sharp features softened a little, and it was almost as if she were talking to Shelley as an equal.

"We shouldn't ever have got married. Vernon

wasn't my type; he never was. I should have known it. He wasn't bad looking when he was younger—quiet of course. I didn't know how sickly he was going to be. He never said anything about that or how sick he'd been as a kid."

"He had rheumatic fever, after the measles. Didn't you know that?" Shelley asked.

Catherine shook her head. "He never told me anything about it. He always treated me like a kid." Her face tightened. "Well, I *was* a kid then, I guess. But he was an old man, right from the time we got married. He never . . . well, performed very well, as a husband, I mean. Let's hope Arlan turns out better that way for you."

Shelley didn't want to hear this about Vernon, and she didn't want Catherine mucking about in her relationship with Arlan either. She started to get up from the table.

"Vernon never took me anywhere," Catherine continued, not noticing Shelley's discomfort and in a voice full of self-pity. "He'd never go to parties or anything. He never took a vacation in his life; he never went anywhere."

"I used to visit Grandmother Joyner with Vernon, though," Shelley said. "I don't think you ever came with us."

"I didn't like his mother," Catherine said roughly. "She didn't like me, either, so I guess that made us even. She thought I gobbled up her precious little boy. Vernon's idea was that all our weekends should be spent with his mother, and I wouldn't go, so we ended up not going anywhere. Not even after she died. Vernon just grubbed along, a nickel here, a nickel there. He didn't know anything else, but he sure knew how to hang on to every cent he had."

And if he hadn't, Shelley thought, where would we be? He'd had so little to dole out. Catherine had never been able to get that one simple fact into her head.

"Vernon was a shock," Catherine mused. "I thought he'd be like my father—I thought men were *all* like my father. That was my big mistake."

"What was your father like?" Shelley asked.

"Oh, he was a prince," Catherine remembered dreamily. "I adored him. He was so wonderful to me. He brought home the most beautiful clothes for me. Even a whole riding habit once, with little jodhpurs and a hat. . . . He'd take me riding. . . . I told you, Axel reminds me of him."

Life had dealt her a lot of cruel blows, Shelley thought. Vernon, New Hope, Sentinel Head. . . .

"The bottom dropped out of my life when he died," Catherine said sadly. "My brothers were gone, and there was no one left but my mother."

"Vernon said the two of you didn't get along very well." Shelley hesitated. Catherine's face locked into anger.

"She hated me," Catherine said. "She was jealous of me, because of my father. She made life a living hell for him. She'd sulk for days when he brought me things, and then she'd light into him. After he died she tried to run my life. Well, she didn't get away with it," she finished angrily.

Shelley looked up without speaking. Catherine's face was twisted with hate.

"She didn't like one of the guys I was going with," Catherine said. "She lit into me, the way she did with Papa. I let her have it, and I took off right after that."

"Is your mother still alive?" Shelley asked. "Vernon took me once to visit her, and all I can remember is that she never seemed to know I was even there. She sat and complained to Vernon the whole time."

"About me, I guess," Catherine commented without much interest. "I never went back, I told you. The boys never bothered to write to me. I don't know if she's alive or not." Catherine was the picture of indifference. Where was the guilt Vernon had talked about? Shelley couldn't see it.

"I've got to get out of here. I've wasted my life," Catherine said bleakly. "Up to now, anyhow, because of Mother and Vernon." She gathered her money from the table and left the kitchen.

And what about me? Shelley wondered. Catherine hadn't listed her along with Vernon and the mother. Probably she should be grateful for that. But it hurt that Catherine hadn't mentioned her at all. Apparently she didn't even count. How could someone who didn't even count anchor down someone who didn't want to stay? How soon would it be before the break came, and what was going to happen to Shelley Joyner when it did?

Shelley walked to the window and checked the wind direction again. The southwest wind was veering to the east, and the early spring would be over. Shelley was enough versed in the vagaries of the weather to anticipate—and fear—a storm.

Chapter 15

BEFORE SHELLEY LEFT FOR SCHOOL THE NEXT DAY, Arlan hammered on the door.

"We're off for a few days to the Banks. Dad wants to get some fishing in while this good weather lasts. I just stopped to say good-bye."

"Aren't you afraid of a storm?" Shelley asked anxiously. "My vane last night was pointing to the southeast."

"That's right," Arlan said. "A small storm system went through last night. But she's back to the west this morning. Dad's got his mind set. Figures the weather'll hold." He kissed her, but the truck was waiting, and she had to let him go.

Shelley checked her wind gauge. This morning it was blowing lightly from the southwest, just as Arlan had said. She set off for the school bus, but in spite of the gauge she didn't like the feel of things. She didn't know why. The southeast looked malevolent—that was all—brooding, and every so often a colder slit of air hit her face. It was almost too hot, and the air was heavy.

At noon there was a perceptible change. The seas coming onto the beach rolled, snarling, not really roaring, and the water had an oily look to it.

"Storm brewer," one of the kids remarked. "Look at the sky." Shelley looked reluctantly into the black face of the southeast.

"Mom said no way was she going to hang out today," a girl commented. Weather vanes were built into the women of the place, and their clothes lines were a far more accurate gauge of the weather than the Halifax radio station. By afternoon the wind and seas had picked up. When Shelley got off the bus after school, the first thing she heard was the roll and crash of the big seas.

Surely the Brock men would have thought better of their fishing and come home. But their truck was not parked beside the house, and Shelley knew that when Axel had set his mind, it took a lot to change it.

When she got home, she found Catherine, her hair glazed into intricate coils and waves, brewing a pot of tea.

"Have you heard a weather report?" Shelley asked.

"There's a gale warning out. That's worse than a storm, they told me. I heard about it in town. Did the Brocks go out?" Catherine asked.

"I guess so. They're not here anyhow," Shelley answered.

"Well, everyone was talking about it. They told Axel not to go, but he was dead set, they say."

"I expect he knows what he's doing," Shelley responded. She hung up her coat and sat down to her tea.

"I told you not to get mixed up with these fishermen," Catherine said. "You spend your life worrying about them, and they're gone all the time anyway. But you wouldn't listen to me."

Shelley, noting the martyred tone, continued to drink her tea. She avoided Catherine's eye, hoping to deflect the conversation, but Catherine wasn't to be turned aside.

"There's something else you'd better listen to me about," she stated ominously. "I hear you've started to walk out on the Head with Arlan. Well, you'd better cut it out."

"Why?" Shelley asked.

"Because you're going to get caught; that's why. You don't know thing one about men, Shelley. You're letting things get ahead of you."

Well, she ought to know, Shelley thought furiously. Leave it to Catherine! At the very moment when she could use a little sympathy and understanding—Arlan out in a storm—here comes Catherine to jump on her with both feet and about something that wasn't even happening.

"I'm not going to get caught," Shelley said between her teeth, "for your information."

"Well, everyone's talking about you," Catherine snapped. "I'm trying to tell you something, but as usual, you won't listen to me."

Listen to her! People all over Port Huyett were talking about Catherine, Janet had said. Shelley gulped her tea.

"And just what are people saying about Arlan and me?" she asked icily.

"You know what they're saying. You aren't that stupid!" Catherine retorted. Her face flushed, and

134

her voice took on a high, excited tone. It further enraged Shelley.

"I don't care what anyone's saying. Or even *if* they're saying it." She stood up, carried her cup to the sink, and thumped it on the drain board. "I'll walk where I want to, with or without Arlan." She started for the stairs.

"Well, don't come bawling to me if you get in trouble," Catherine yelled. "Because I'm not going to bail you out. I'm not about to raise your babies."

Shelley stopped at the foot of the stairs and looked back into the kitchen. Catherine, her face ablaze, sat at the table. A gust of wind slammed into the house. She jumped, frightened, and looked fearfully out the window.

"Don't worry, Catherine," Shelley said, "raising my children is one thing I'll never ask you to do. When and if I have them, it's going to be because I want them." She walked upstairs, not waiting to see, not wanting to learn, whether her words in any way matched Catherine's fear of the oncoming storm.

The storm roared in from the sea at precisely 4:37. It was Shelley's first real gale, and in spite of all the tales she had been told, she was not prepared for its ferocity. No one had warned her that the full blast of its onslaught would batter the house, literally shaking it, like some animal in the jaws of a predator. She hadn't known that lightning, thunder, rain, hail, would hurl themselves in succession at the land, that the wind would shriek and howl, and that above all the din, each roar and explosion of each huge sea as it hit the shore would drown out every other sound.

Shelley came downstairs and managed a supper of sorts, though the electric power was long gone. Catherine, terrified by the storm, cringed in the flickering candlelight.

"Will the house hold out?" She turned toward Shelley like a small child and looked up, pleading, into her face. "Should we leave?"

"We can't go out in this," Shelley responded crossly. "Don't be ridiculous. We'd be blown off the face of the earth." She glanced again at Catherine's huddled, trembling body.

"Axel told me this was a sturdy house and would stand up to any storm," she said more gently. "Why don't you take one of your pills and crawl into bed, where it's warmer. I don't want to light the stove in this wind. I won't be going to bed anyhow; I'll take care of things."

Most of the night Shelley sat at her window, as if her presence there held some kind of magical staying power. At times she started to drop off to sleep in exhaustion but was immediately startled into wakefulness by some new and unbelievable attack against the house.

No little boat could survive in such a storm; yet Shelley's mind, while telling her that this was so, could not couple that fact with the loss of Arlan and his family. The brutality of the storm numbed her. She didn't know how she endured the night, for over and over in her mind she actually saw Arlan's boat go down.

The storm abated toward morning, and Shelley,

sick at heart, dressed and went downstairs to put on her coat. She would have to face Dru sooner or later.

Outside, she was buffeted by the wind, which seemed to come from every direction, and half crying, she fought her way to the Brocks and pounded on the door. Arlan opened it and stood horrified in the doorway when he saw her.

"ARLAN!" Shelley fell into his arms. She'd lost her father so recently, and this second loss, even in imagination, was beyond any holding in. She cried harder than she ever had in her life and soaked Arlan's shirt front with her tears.

"How could you possibly think we'd be out in that?" Arlan scolded. "Do you think we're nuts?"

"What difference does it make whether you were out or not?" Dru turned angrily on Arlan. "Shelley's lived through a storm with you out at sea. You haven't the first idea what that means. None of you men do."

Arlan looked as crestfallen as if Dru had slapped his face. He brought Shelley to the table and wordlessly held out a chair for her. Axel, who was already seated, looked down at his plate. There was a guilty silence around the table.

"I'm sorry, Shelley. We sometimes forget," Arlan said.

"I guess breakfast with you guys is what you call a port in a storm or something," Shelley ventured, her voice shaking and sounding water soaked. "I'm sorry for all the fuss. Arlan, I've got your shirt all wet."

Arlan flapped his shirt front. "I'll go hang myself on the clothes line," he said, with a rueful look at

Dru. Shelley laughed as suddenly as she had cried and with about the same degree of relief.

"We have warning these days of foul weather," Axel gently explained. "You'd not likely be caught out in a gale like that unless your radio went out or you had engine trouble and couldn't get in. The worst that happens these days is that you lose your gear." He looked over at Dru. "In years past there have been plenty of times when the men were caught. Dru's been all through it. This storm came in rather sudden, and she was a bad one. Could have expected her, though, after all the warm weather this early."

"Arlan, you'd better tell Shelley where you were all day," Dru said. "We should have thought to tell you yesterday afternoon. I suppose you noticed that the truck was gone."

"We drove up to Halifax," Arlan said quietly, though his eyes shone, "and I signed up for the Coast Guard. They were filling up a quota, so I even took the physical. I'll be leaving tomorrow morning."

"That's wonderful, Arlan." Shelley meant it. She was going to be happy about it if it killed her, if her heart broke in a thousand pieces at the thought of his going away.

There was a clumping in the mud room, and Clyde came in. "Ah, a second breakfast!" he shouted. "Hello, Shelley. Some blow," and to Axel, "She's headed nor'east, and it's getting cold. Arlan, you ought to take Shelley out on the Head and show her what a real sea is like."

"But I have school, and anyway wouldn't you three be going out if the weather is clearing?"

"In *this?*" Arlan asked incredulously.

"Well, you will in the Coast Guard if you have to rescue somebody," Shelley pointed out and noted with amusement that Arlan looked mighty thoughtful. "Oh!" She jumped up. "My bus!"

"You've already missed it," Arlan said. "So why don't you just skip school and come on out on the Head with me? It's our last day together for a while."

"I've never played hooky before," Shelley said, thinking suddenly of Vernon. He didn't go for playing hooky, but he'd have understood this, with Arlan leaving and all. She never gave a thought to Catherine.

"Better put on my old windbreak, Shelley. It'll go over your jacket, and you'll need it against the wind. Here's a hat, too," Arlan said, handing her a wool cap with a tassel. Shelley almost disappeared inside these gigantic pieces of clothing.

The Head was beautiful. The sky was filled with jagged, black clouds, occasionally silvery or lined with silver as an intermittent sun caught them, and they raced frantically before the wind. It was cold. The wind would have penetrated any wool garment, no matter how thick. Their windbreaks, designed for work at sea, blocked it but offered a surface to push against, and even with Arlan tugging at Shelley and steadying her from time to time, they had a struggle to break through to land's end. As they neared the point, the gusts were too powerful altogether, and

139

Shelley dropped to her hands and knees and crawled from rock to rock, clutching the crags and hanging on for dear life. The wind even pushed against her eyelids and blurred her vision.

Shelley tried to shout at Arlan, but the thunder of the breaking seas made any attempt at talk futile. In any case, the spectacle was too huge for chatter. It was as if the rollers, even though the storm was over, had to continue the news of a disturbance far out at sea. Arlan steered Shelley into a protected cleft in the rocks and then along a stony ledge into a cavity, a sort of cave, with space for two. Shelley, gasping for breath, sat down close beside him. Outside the cold wind howled, but it passed by them and over their heads. The rocks somewhat muffled the roar of the sea, and she and Arlan could talk without shouting.

But they didn't talk. Instead, huddled together in exhaustion after the strenuous climb, they both grew warm. They took off their windbreaks and finally even their heavy jackets, and after that they sank into a mutual pleasure in the nearness of their bodies. Arlan put his arms around Shelley. It was the ultimate haven, the safe harbour from all the tempests of the year, a delicious comfort, and they sat quietly for a time, sinking into it.

But it was too easy, and in Shelley's mind flashed a persistent signal of danger. Still she was captive to Arlan's warmth and her own yearning, and when he unbuttoned her shirt and began to feel his slow, quiet way between the layers of her clothing, she couldn't bring herself to stop him.

140

"Arlan!" she whispered, grabbing, but not staying his hand, "should we . . ."

"Let's go on, Shelley," he said, kissing her and then kissing her again more urgently. She let him, almost dreamily. She thought of Janet, and again of Arlan's careful plans, but these were miles away and didn't matter any more. Nothing did, except Arlan and her wanting of him.

It was so natural the way he did it that she hardly noticed when he eased her against the stone ledge and laid his own body beside and partly over hers. She'd never been so happy, so content. But as if she had been caught in a riptide, an unexpected force carried her beyond the quiet loving into a fierceness that she couldn't control. All her wanting of Arlan hit her at once and swept her away. She didn't care—nothing could stop them, not any sort of warning, nor threats to their future, no thoughts of family except . . .

Catherine! Shelley tried to push her mother out of her mind, but she wouldn't go. It was as if she had waved in front of Shelley's eyes every promise she'd made to Vernon, every vow to herself that she wouldn't be caught like Catherine. "See! I told you so!" Catherine shouted vindictively. Shelley frantically resisted, but Catherine overwhelmed her, stamping on all that was private between her and Arlan and extinguishing their love as if it had been a brushfire under her feet.

With a tremendous effort of will, since every part of her was shrieking yes, Shelley pushed Arlan away. "Arlan, no!" she gasped and stood up. Crying and blinded, she fumbled with the buttons of her shirt. She grabbed her jacket and tried to get into it, then bolted out into the wind with it half on, half off, her windbreak dragging on the ground. Arlan followed. He grabbed her by the shoulders. His face was red and angry, and he shook her so that it hurt.

"Shelley," he shouted furiously above the sea's clamor, "don't you *ever* do that to me again!"

They walked across the moor without speaking, the wind pushing them, until they came to her house.

"I'm sorry, Arlan," Shelley whispered.

"If you loved me, you'd *never* have done that to me!" he said; and not looking back, he strode off down the road.

A furious Catherine flung the door open.

"Where have you been?" she yelled. "Why aren't you in school?"

"I was out on the Head, with Arlan," Shelley said dully, walking in. She was disheveled, her windbreak clutched in one hand, her jacket ill buttoned, her shirt still in bunches where Arlan had pulled at it. She couldn't absorb the rest of Catherine's tirade. She couldn't recognize herself in the stream of epithets and invective that she heard. Once she heard Catherine call her a slut.

"You can't be trusted for one single minute!" Catherine shrieked. "We're getting out of here. Tomorrow. We're selling out and going back to New Hope."

Shelley did hear this. Every word. And understood its meaning. Its threat. She'd lost Arlan at the moment when she most loved him and wanted him, had done so because of the shrieking fury before her. And now she was to lose Sentinel Head as well.

Shelley turned to her mother and fixed her eyes on Catherine's face. She rolled up a lifetime of Catherine's failures and threw them at her, accusing her with her stare and intentionally summoning guilt. Catherine faltered and fell silent.

"I'm not leaving," Shelley stated. "You can do what you want. But you get out of my life, Catherine," she said steadily. "And you stay out of it."

Chapter 16

HOME WAS INTOLERABLE, SO SHELLEY HITCHED A ride into town, where she spent an agonized afternoon at school. Catherine was not there when she got back. Surely Arlan would come in the evening, and they would make things right. But as the hours crept by, he didn't come, and eventually, exhausted, she fell into bed.

Early in the morning, Arlan knocked on the front door, and Shelley opened it. He had to leave, he said hurriedly; he'd raced up to say good-bye, but Axel was waiting in the truck. He put his arm around Shelley, but when she looked up into his face, she saw that it was filled with misery. She had hurt him, more than she had even thought.

"Shelley, I wish I could make you understand—"
Arlan said. He couldn't seem to find the right words,
and the sentence was left hanging.

But he had to be breaking everything up. How
else could she interpret what he was saying. What
she'd done to him had been so cruel, so rejecting.
Shelley didn't know how to to explain that Catherine—*Catherine!*—had come between them. And
there wasn't time. Axel honked the truck horn.

"Arlan," she said desperately. The truck horn
sounded another warning.

"We've *got* to leave, Shelley. We're already late.
I'll write you." He kissed her, but it was hurried and
told her nothing, nothing at least that she wanted to
know. He turned back as he crawled into the truck
to look at her and wave, but all she could see was his
face still full of worry and distress.

Shelley went back into the house. She didn't
know Arlan well enough to be absolutely sure what
he was thinking, what he meant by "I wish I could
make you understand," but it was impossible to believe the fire was not out on the hearth, and that she
had not quenched it herself.

As she had quenched any hope of accommodation between herself and Catherine, any hope of
Catherine's adjustment to Sentinel Head. Catherine
took Shelley at her word and spent most of her days
in town and then some nights as well. Shelley suffered through the nights in an agony of worry.
Where was she? Would she come back? She com-
posed countless little speeches with which to confront Catherine when she returned, but when she
showed up cold and obviously defiant, Shelley in her

turn studiously ignored her. When the two of them were together in the house, there was no conversation other than the most perfunctory. As late April's return to winter became intolerable, so the isolation between herself and Catherine, even as they occupied the same small space in the kitchen, was almost unendurable and ended in guilt and self-recrimination—for Shelley, at least. If Catherine suffered, she showed no sign of it.

Shelley couldn't stand the empty house. It made no difference whether Catherine was in it or not; it was still empty, and for the next couple of weeks, in desperation, Shelley walked down to the Brocks in the evenings. On one of those evenings, Dru, after a few minutes of chat, asked, "What's the matter, Shelley? Arlan looked so miserable just before he left, and you look almost as bad. Is there anything wrong between the two of you?"

"I don't know, Dru," Shelley answered slowly. She needed someone to talk to, not only about Arlan but also about Catherine. But Dru, perhaps misreading the signals, merely patted her hand.

"Lovers' quarrels," she said almost absently. "They soon pass."

Dru was absorbed in getting ready for what Shelley thought must be one of the most exciting events of her life. Arlan had left, her last fledgling from the nest, and she and Axel were taking off on an extended visit to family. The lobstering had been good, and they had bought a new car. Dru was putting the house in storage as if the trip were to last for months rather than the scheduled three weeks. Shelley was delighted for them and envied them as well.

They would go first to the Valley, taking with them Clyde and also Gail, who had a week off from the bank where she worked. Then, after returning the young couple to Sentinel Head, they would go alone by ferry to Newfoundland. Every day for them would be like Janet's wedding, the greeting of old friends and family, the pleasure in their company, chatting and fun. Shelley helped with the preparations, but in her heart she knew that Sentinel Head was going to be one lonely place without them.

"Heard from Arlan?" Axel said as he came into the kitchen. In the fish shed and on his boat, he was duplicating Dru's frenzied activities. The nets must be dried. He had them strung out along the road edge. He couldn't get past his new car in the driveway but stopped what he was doing, over and over, to open the hood and examine some part of the engine, to crawl in the front seat in order to study the dashboard.

"I haven't heard one word from Arlan," Shelley said.

Axel responded almost as absently as Dru had earlier. "Oh well, boot camp."

Shelley got up from the table and took her jacket down from the row of pegs by the kitchen door.

"I do wonder what he's doing, though," she said.

"Bending his head, I expect," Axel pointed out. "That's a full-time occupation for Arlan. He don't like people telling him what to do, and if he gets started on something, he sure don't like to be interrupted. Once he gets up a head of steam, it takes him a long time to cool down and forget about it. Forgive and forget but always remember; that's Arlan."

"I guess you're right," Shelley said sadly and let herself out the door. It would take Arlan a long time to forgive, and even if he tried to forget, maybe he would never manage to do it.

Shelley found a letter from Arlan in the mailbox the next afternoon when she got home from school. Taking it inside—no sign of Catherine—Shelley sat down on the daybed in the empty living room and opened the envelope. It was a single sheet of what looked like school notebook paper, written in pencil in Arlan's cramped, uneasy hand:

Dear Shelley,

I don't know what time it is anymore, I don't know if it's night or day they keep after you every minute. I go to church on Sunday, it's the only time you hear a kind word. I wish you had a telephone, I'd try to call you. I wish I could explain everything.

I hate to think about us. Everything was going so right. Now it seems like my whole life's changed, because of what happened and it looks like every minute is going to be used up by the service for the rest of my life, nothing else matters anymore.

I have to go.

> Love,
> Arlan

The message was clear enough. Anyone could read through Arlan's awkward phrases to the truth. "I hate to think about us"—about us busting up, Shelley interpreted. "My whole life's changed" and I don't need you anymore. ". . . the service for the rest of my life" without you . . . "nothing else matters anymore," especially not you, Shelley . . . "I wish I could explain," but you don't need to, Arlan, I've got the message.

Shelley walked into the kitchen. Carefully lifting a sheet of paper from her notebook, she wrote:

Dear Arlan,
    I wish it hadn't turned out that way. It was a terrible mistake, and I think I was the one who made it. All I can say is I'm terribly sorry.
    I really hope you get to like the Coast Guard better and that it gives you the kind of life you want.
    You were awfully nice to me, Arlan.
                    Love,
                      Shelley

She got an envelope and stamp from Vernon's dresser, where he had kept his few business items, and then, copying the address, she took the letter up the road and dropped it in the Crawford box. The mail lady didn't always come down to the end of the road, not if there was nothing to deliver, and, besides, having the flag up on the mailbox would alert Catherine. Even if she didn't open the letter, and Shelley didn't think she would, still it was hard to believe she wouldn't surmise what was in it, wouldn't know somehow. Shelley's heart was breaking, but it was not possible that Catherine should know it.

Shelley didn't tell Dru about the letter, either. For the two days before they left, Shelley went about her routine—school, housekeeping, shopping for groceries, and helping Dru get ready—fiercely numbing herself against any feeling as she did so, determined not to spoil any of the Brocks' vacation. Time enough when they got back.

On the morning of their departure, Shelley waved an enthusiastic if hypocritical good-bye. Three weeks would be an eternity. She would water Dru's plants and feed the cat. The cat was an outdoor tom, claiming his food ration only if nothing better showed up. He didn't even have a name, and Shelley couldn't see that he filled much of a role in the household. She didn't expect companionship from the cat in any case, and as the car left, the cat's yellow eyes watching from the wood pile didn't offer any.

Getting off had proved difficult for the usually organized Brocks: They were behind schedule, and Shelley had finally dispatched them, promising to wash up after their hurried breakfast. The house seemed terribly quiet without them, and she wished they'd left any day but Saturday. The weekend stretched endlessly ahead, lonely and empty. As she was locking up, Shelley saw Catherine coming toward her, on her way to town. She saw Shelley standing there on the doorstep—there was no way she couldn't have seen her—but she stalked straight ahead, making no sign.

Shelley walked slowly home, to the unanswering kitchen and brewed herself a cup of coffee. There was a quick rap at the kitchen door, and Janet walked in.

"Janet!" Shelley jumped up and made a grab in the air as if her friend were going to disappear before her eyes. "You can't think how *glad* I am to see you!"

"Well, me, too," Janet responded. "I want to talk to you. Listen, is Catherine here?" she asked in a low voice. Shelley shook her head.

"Off to town. As usual," she added bitterly. "We're not doing too well together."

"Let's have a cup of coffee," Janet suggested. "I can smell it, so I know you have some."

They sat down at the table. "Are you missing Arlan a lot?" Janet asked.

Shelley smiled a little. Janet hadn't come to ask about Arlan. More likely it was Catherine. You didn't show up this early in the morning to ask if your chum were lonely for her boyfriend.

"Of course I'm missing him," Shelley answered. She thought, wistfully, of telling Janet about Arlan, what she'd done to him, about the letters, his and hers, but it was too private, too full of pain, and there was Janet herself, the lovable chatterbox. . . . It was going to be hard to keep her at arm's length, though.

For a minute they sat and looked at each other. They sipped their coffee, and neither of them said a word. Finally Janet drew a long breath.

150

"Being married is really wonderful, Shelley," Janet said.

"Well, you haven't been at it very long," Shelley pointed out.

Janet laughed. "Just the same, we've decided to start a family. As soon as we can find a place to live. Craig's Dad's trailer is OK for us—it's sort of fun, like playing house. But there sure isn't room for a baby."

"Where will you look?" Shelley asked.

"Craig doesn't make that much, you know, Shelley. It's going to be hard to find *anyplace* we can afford and still save up for a house of our own. Life really keeps your nose to the grindstone, doesn't it?" Janet moaned.

Shelley smiled a little. It *was* going to be hard for them. But at least Janet had Craig, someone who belonged to her.

"I was afraid you might be jealous of us," Janet confessed. "I mean with Arlan gone and Catherine acting the way she is."

"What *is* Catherine up to?" Shelley asked, steering Janet to the point. "I've got to know the people around here pretty well, the kids and everything, but I don't know who the people are she's hanging out with at the Dragger."

"Well, Craig goes over there with the guys sometimes. He likes a game of pool—the gang he goes with are mostly the fellers just in from sea. They're OK." Shelley nodded again. Janet could take her time, all weekend if necessary.

"There's a man comes in a lot, Roy Manning. His folks live in town. His mother's not too good, and Roy's up—from Florida, I think." Janet hesitated and glanced quickly over at Shelley. Shelley continued to sip her coffee.

"Well, Catherine's . . . going with him. I mean, they're together all the time. They even—" Janet stopped abruptly.

"Catherine doesn't always come home nights," Shelley said evenly. "I've known something was going on for a long time. Even Vernon knew, but he just stopped caring."

"Well, Roy's only been here for a couple of months," Janet said, "and it's only lately you see her around town in the evenings. They don't make any bones about it—they're crazy about each other."

"What's he like?"

"Well, he's not my type, and I don't guess he's yours. He's rough, not really mean, though, Craig says. Big feller. He had a bar down south and brags about it a lot," Janet explained. "He's made a lot of money, Craig says." She hesitated and looked uneasy.

"Shelley, I just want to say something, and maybe I shouldn't, but I think Roy's just what Catherine's been looking for all this time. He's just her type. You'll be a lot happier if you just recognize that, instead of—" Janet stopped.

"Instead of what?" Shelley asked.

"Well, you keep trying to turn Catherine into something she isn't." Janet looked downright miserable but determined.

"You always got along with her," Shelley said. "It made me awfully jealous. But I guess you could just shrug and say to yourself, 'Well, crazy old Catherine,' and let it go at that." Shelley's voice shook, and she got up and walked over to the stove.

"What's left for her here?" Janet pleaded. "Honestly. She's awfully lonely, for men anyhow. She's never really gotten along with the women around here the way you have. Craig says you should just see her at the Dragger. She's a different person."

Shelley looked over Janet's head and out the living room window to the sea beyond. Janet was right, and she ought to have accepted the fact a long time ago. Catherine herself didn't make any bones about it, never had. She'd mooned around about men, any man, for years, unable to detach herself from Vernon. Not that Shelley Joyner was all that different. She'd done her share of mooning, she supposed. After tagging around behind Jeanne-Louise all those years, she'd finally found Arlan.

And lost him.

"What's she going to do with her life anyhow?" Janet continued. "She needs a man. She's needed one for a long time. She knows it's just a matter of time till you go off with Arlan."

Arlan! Arlan! Shelley fixed her eyes on the sea. Janet jumped up—she had to leave. She'd promised Granny-mum she'd be right back, but she stopped in the doorway.

"I didn't mean to hurt you, Shelley. But you do everything better than Catherine does. She doesn't have anything."

"You didn't really hurt me, Janet," Shelley responded. "You gave me something to think about, though. It was pretty gutsy of you to come and talk to me like that. And I'm really excited about your having a baby soon." Janet, with another of her flashing smiles, slipped out the door.

Shelley continued to sit at the kitchen table, thinking, and trying not to be angry at Janet. She had a lot of questions to ask, and no one, not even Janet, could answer them. Why was she responsible for Catherine, anyhow? Why had Vernon boxed her in the way he had? When you came down to it, what had she really done to Arlan? Where did she fit into this business with Roy Manning? And why was life knocking her around like this?

Chapter 17

CATHERINE DIDN'T COME HOME THAT SATURDAY and not during the entire weekend. Shelley cleaned house. Not because the house was terribly in want of an overhaul, but because something made her do it, a sense that a phase of her life had come, or was coming, to an end, and she'd better be ready for it. She didn't touch Catherine's things and never once entered her room, but she finally laid to rest the last vestiges of Vernon's life, the few artifacts left in his dresser drawer, which had been pending division between herself and Catherine. The time had come, and if Catherine didn't want the things, well, OK. Shelley took them upstairs, a little worked leather box, a paperweight, a polished wooden hairbrush she'd always admired, though the bristles were too soft, and a quite nice pair of cuff links, apparently never worn, for they were still attached to the original cardboard. Shelley wondered who had given them to Vernon.

After that, and lacking other occupation, she also did a magnificently thorough job on her homework. If things went on like this, she thought grimly, she'd end up the school's honor student. On Sunday she walked out on the Head, and discovering Old Jaimie, gave him a hand with his chores. He'd stopped arguing about it, a long time ago, and when she brought along a new loaf, as she often did, she enjoyed watching his stern face light up.

"Been crippled up some this week," he said with a half smile. "I take it kindly." He looked old and in lots of pain. He wasn't going to last forever, Shelley thought in sadness.

She was glad when Monday came—still no Catherine—and she could get away from the empty house and back to school. It did not please her at all as it did the others, when the school boiler, old, in urgent need of repair, broke down, as it had several times during the winter, and everyone was sent home early.

When Shelley opened her house door—it was unlocked and Catherine must have returned—she was greeted by a collection of suitcases, boxes, and parcels in the hall. Catherine's two coats were flung over the lot: Her departure was obviously imminent. Catherine herself stood in the kitchen, trapped, her face showing a rapid succession of anger, alarm, and guilt and then a combination of all three.

"I take it you're leaving," Shelley said coldly. She put her books on the table and faced her—mother.

"There isn't anything here for me, and you know it," Catherine answered defiantly.

"I gather I don't count." Shelley looked at—through—Catherine, but this time Catherine didn't turn away.

"You told me to get out of your life. Anyway, you can take care of yourself," she said. "You always have."

"There's always the fish plant, I suppose," Shelley responded. Catherine didn't move. Not one muscle in her face moved. It could have been carved in granite.

"I started to work at sixteen. In a factory," she countered. "Anyway, you have Vernon's pension. At least for a while."

Shelley continued to stare, unbelieving. Catherine had left her mother, she'd run away at sixteen, and here she was, at forty plus, doing it all over again, only this time Shelley was the parent, Catherine still the child. Shelley wondered if Catherine's mother had tried to stop her. Probably. Catherine had told her off, Shelley remembered. Well, Catherine isn't going to tell *me* off, Shelley decided. She'd keep the lid on if it killed her. And if Catherine wanted to go, let her.

"I assume, from reports," Shelley said in as even a voice as she could manage, "that you're taking off with this Roy Manning. Am I going to have a chance to meet him?"

"He doesn't want to be involved," Catherine

responded. "We didn't know you'd be coming home early."

"Very neat," Shelley commented. "You were careful to pick a time when Axel was out of the way, too. That was smart of you." This apparently hit home, for Catherine winced.

"You have Arlan," she said defensively. Shelley didn't answer. Catherine began to whine, on the unpleasant note she always used. "Well, *you've* always done what you wanted to. Now I'm going to live the way *I* want to. For a change. You—"

Shelley continued to stare at her, but this couldn't go on. Catherine would not stay in control of herself much longer; her defenses were crumbling fast. After that would come her cruel invective, a helpless tantrum. And Shelley didn't want to cope with it again, not after the last sickening scene between them. "Do you need money?" she asked abruptly.

"Roy's going to take care of me. He's loaded." Catherine tossed her head. "He said I probably have dower rights to the pension and the house, too, even if Vernon left them to you. But Roy says you can have them. For now."

"Thanks a lot," Shelley said coldly. She didn't know about these things, but Vernon surely had, and in any case the solicitor would help her. Right now she didn't care.

Shelley opened her handbag. It was nearing the end of the month, and Catherine had already had her share of the funds, but Shelley took out half of what remained and laid it on the table.

157

"Mad money," she said shortly. Catherine picked it up.

"I'm not coming back," she said. "No matter what."

Shelley merely nodded, forcing back the "Well, who wants you?" that had almost escaped. "Are you going to take your plants?" she asked.

"I don't want them," Catherine replied.

Shelley heard a car pull up in front of the house.

"He doesn't want to be involved," Catherine repeated.

"I can see why," Shelley said. "Are you going to leave an address or anything?"

Catherine didn't answer at first. "We don't want to be tracked down, by you or Axel or anyone else," she said. "And I mean it. For your information, his folks don't know where we'll be either. Anyhow, you told me to stay out of your life."

"I'll go upstairs, then," Shelley said quietly. She took her purse and climbed over the luggage at the foot of the stairs. "Good luck," she made herself say from the stairs and was not surprised when Catherine didn't answer. The upstairs windows faced the sea, not the street. Shelley sat on her bed until she heard the car shift gears and leave. She never even got a glimpse of Roy Manning.

Shelley stalked downstairs and made straight for Catherine's windowsill of plants. Seizing a coleus and grasping it at the stem, she yanked it out of the pot and hurled it with all her force on the floor. It hadn't been watered, and the whole clump crumpled into dirt, leaving the roots clinging to bits of damper soil. She left the plant on the floor and bolted out the door, slamming it behind her.

Shelley first ran blindly; then she slowed and finally walked stolidly out to the Head, all the way to the point. She sat on the rocks where she and Arlan had struggled with the storm, and she numbly watched the gulls lined up in formal rows on a spit of rocks across from her. For a moment, forgetting, she smiled.

"Great was the company of the preachers." The phrase came into her mind, making her suddenly lonely for Vernon, who had laughed at the chanting chorus on the radio, just before he had made her promise to take care of Catherine.

Well, she hadn't taken care of Catherine; she'd failed, and her loneliness turned to guilt, which every day was sickening her a little more, and then to anger. Anger against Vernon. Against Catherine, both of them. She sat there on the hard rock, the sea crashing in front of her, too angry to cry, too furious even to feel panic at Catherine's abandonment of her. With an effort, she began then, to assess her situation. What was to become of Shelley Joyner, aged sixteen, a minor, with no available relatives? The possibilities were not encouraging.

She couldn't write Arlan into her life, not anymore. And because of that, Axel and Dru. How would it look for them to take in Arlan's ex-girlfriend? She couldn't ask them.

Janet and Craig were already cramped in their tiny trailer, and if things went as planned, there would be a baby.

The Crawfords, no. Not even Granny-mum. Too many problems there already.

For a moment she thought, with sadness, of old Jaimie.

Phoebe Crandall. She could work at the hotel. But Phoebe was Brock family, and it would be presuming.

School. The school people would insist on finding Catherine and bringing her back. It was the law. Even though Shelley was perfectly willing to stay alone on Sentinel Head, they wouldn't let her, a minor. No use trying to keep Catherine's abandonment secret either. It would be all over town.

Shelley even considered her distant cousin in Digby, but the cousin was an old lady, Jaimie's age; why should she take on a distant relative? Billy, her half-brother, she *refused* to consider.

Her mind kept coming back to Phoebe Crandall. If she had a job at the hotel . . . She could do the work. Arlan had said so. "Of course you could, Shelley!" he'd said. Phoebe had taken in the motorcycle boy and a lot of other kids.

Why not Shelley Joyner, even if she had busted up with Phoebe's favorite nephew? Her mind turned on the question and turned some more and kept on turning. She didn't *know* what to do, and she was sick with the anger inside her. She'd tried; everybody, every single thing, life itself, had let her down. She looked for a long time out to sea, watching the incoming waves, the endless progression, and listening to the rhythm of their beating against the rocks below her.

What did the sea have to say about loneliness? Nothing. It couldn't care less. She could panic, she could scream and yell with rage; it wouldn't care. If there was one lesson you learned out here, from sea and land, it was that nothing you did made any difference at all. The indifference was total, and you had to accept it.

You had to accept it. Shelley sat up and looked in surprise at the sea, as if it had suddenly tossed a shell or a ball of spindrift into her lap. *Accept.*

She'd seen Old Jaimie turn and look seaward; she'd caught him looking over the heads of the people at Vernon's grave, his eyes on the sea beyond. His face would sadden, as if he were checking once more, asking once more, and the answer was always the same; it has to be.

You had to accept that some things would happen, no matter what you did, that you, frail thing, had no power to stop them. Vernon had died. Catherine had run away. Maybe that was what growing up was all about, that you knew things would happen and you accepted the fact, as Dru and Phoebe had accepted death, as Axel accepted the hardships of life at sea. You had to bend your head, he kept telling Arlan.

It was the lesson of the sea and land, she thought, of the whole world around her, and she was lucky Vernon had brought her here to learn it. How could she ever have heard the message in No-Hope?

* * *

A fishing boat, a trawler, like Axel's boat, like the ones Arlan and most of the guys she knew worked on, appeared on the far horizon to her left. The fisherman would be coming from Port Huyett harbor and angling westward, keeping well away from treacherous Sentinel Head. Shelley liked to watch the stubnosed trawlers. You could see them batting their way through the seas, like street kids with their fists doubled up. They were tough and independent, like the fishermen in them.

Fishermen, though, were not above asking for help when the going got rough. Axel relied on all kinds of help, sonar to read the water depth, radar so that someone could locate him if he was lost, radio and Ship to Shore, and there was the Coast Guard in the background, watchful of its brood. The fishermen weren't helpless these days, Axel had said.

Shelley watched the cocky little boat disappear over the horizon. The fisherman could rage at a storm, but that wouldn't help much. He could sit there stubbornly in his boat, refusing help till he sank. But he wouldn't.

If you asked for help, it was because you were willing to bend your head, you'd learned that things are as they are; you'd understood that you can't afford to be pigheaded, the way Arlan said she was.

She started to cry.

Shelley felt, rather than heard, Old Jaimie limp up the rise behind her. He stood looking down at her.

"My mother's taken off and left me," Shelley sobbed.

"I saw her leave with Manning," he said shortly.

"And I've broken up with Arlan, and I really

don't know why." Shelley couldn't seem to stop crying; she cried even harder. Old Jaimie didn't answer right away. She supposed he was looking out to sea.

"Well, now," he said at last. "You'd best let me take you home."

Chapter 18

"I'LL BE ALL RIGHT, JAIMIE. SORRY," SHELLEY gulped. They walked back to the sheep barn together, she climbed into the truck, and Jaimie drove her home in silence. It was clear he felt well over his head in the present circumstances. Shelley opened the truck door but sat on for a minute. It wasn't right to leave him like this. "Everything just hit me at once, Jaimie. I'll be all right. I'm going in to see Mrs. Luddington in the morning. She'll know how to cope."

Jaimie hesitated. "About you and Arlan . . ." he probed gruffly, embarrassed.

"We had a—misunderstanding. He wrote me a letter from the base, and I wrote him one back," Shelley said. "It's all broken up, I guess. Maybe if I could have talked to him . . ." she added sadly. "He's not very good at writing."

"Sure you'll be all right?" Jaimie asked doubtfully. "When's Axel due back?"

Shelley shook her head. "I'm OK. Really. They're just over in the Valley. They're bringing

Clyde and Gail back in a couple of days, and then they're going on to Newfoundland."

Jaimie continued to look doubtful. "Sure now?"

"Sure." Shelley got out, Jaimie noisily shifted gears, and the truck lurched down the road.

The first thing Shelley saw when she walked into the kitchen was the plant on the floor. She stood looking at it for some time, and then she bent down and picked it up. Had she killed it? She put the coleus back in the pot, scooped the dirt up from the floor and pressed it back around the roots, then watered it and left it to drain in the sink. While she was at it, she watered the rest of the plants.

Catherine hadn't wanted them anymore. What she meant was, she hadn't needed them—her plants, her one area of authority, the one place in the family where she was boss. She'd made them grow only because *she* needed them, not because they needed her. She'd heartlessly let them go dry and then simply walked out on them.

Vernon had said Catherine wasn't much of a mother, that she'd never grown up. But maybe, as Janet said, there were people like that. Still, did she have a right to run away? Shelley absently looked down into Catherine's plants. She began to pull the brown, curled-up leaves off the stems. She could spend her life hating Catherine, using up all her energy in futile attempts to tamp down her anger, letting it spill over onto Vernon and even Arlan. But there had to be a time to stop tearing herself apart.

Catherine usually kept the plants pinched back to rounded masses in their pots, but in the last weeks of neglect they had produced shoots and stringers.

164

Still without focusing much on what her hands were doing, Shelley pinched off the softer coleus and then fetched a pair of scissors from the kitchen drawer to cut back the tougher ivys and piggybacks.

It would have been nice to think that Catherine had abandoned her because it was better for both of them, that she believed it would free Shelley from responsibility. But that wasn't the way it was. Catherine had never put either Vernon's or Shelley's interests above her own. She was still, and always had been, a little girl, craving favor, and from a man.

Deep in thought, Shelley saw her hands, almost as if they belonged to someone else, working among the plants. She would care for the plants instinctively. That was the difference between her and Catherine.

On the school bus the next morning, Shelley could tell from the banter of the kids that word had not gotten around yet about Catherine's leaving. But it would and soon. Shelley sat with the girls, who chattered all around her, but she hadn't the heart to join in. She went immediately to the principal's office and asked to see Mrs. Luddington.

"She's—" began the secretary, but Mrs. Luddington's deep voice interrupted. "Shelley?" she called through the door.

"Mrs. Luddington," Shelley said desperately. "It's an SOS. Like the fishing boats."

"In that case," Sarah Luddington said, coming to the door, "we'll put out after you. In the meantime, you'd better come and tell me about it."

Shelley walked into the office and slid into the chair Mrs. Luddington indicated, releasing her backpack and dropping it to the floor. Mrs. Luddington sat down at her desk and waited.

"My mother ran away yesterday," Shelley said bluntly. "She went off with someone from the Dragger. I've broken up with Arlan, and I don't know what to do."

"It sounds as if you could do with some help," Mrs. Luddington said.

"I guess I ought to tell you what's been happening all this time," Shelley suggested. Her voice shook in spite of her efforts to control it.

If Shelley had thought that the telling would be easy, or if she'd skipped over or even hidden pieces of it or told it untruthfully, she'd have been dead wrong. With Mrs. Luddington's clear eye on her, the whole story came out, complete, unvarnished, and true. Up to the breakup with Arlan, Mrs. Luddington mostly just listened, with short, pointed questions; but when Shelley explained about Arlan, it was different. She was haltingly trying to describe the incident on Sentinel Head when Mrs. Luddington suddenly laughed.

"Oh, for goodness' sakes," she said. "Arlan wasn't killed! What did he expect? Neither of you were prepared, I gather. *Somebody* has to exercise a little control, or we'd all be running around like alley cats."

At first Shelley couldn't take in what Mrs. Luddington was saying. The office walls seemed to shift a little and waver. She stared at Mrs. Luddington, unable to utter a word.

166

"He's probably horribly embarrassed. Making love out there on a pile of rocks! Remember, I know Arlan, too. I know very well he likes to do things right. If he had everything planned out, as I bet he had, he made a horrible goof and doesn't know how to handle it. What did he say in his letter to you, if you don't mind telling me?" Mrs. Luddington asked.

Shelley, her mind still reeling, tried to reconstruct the letter. She'd read it over and over, memorized it, but from this new direction, it actually made sense for the first time. "He—he—I never thought about him feeling guilty, Mrs. Luddington. I suppose that's what he was trying to tell me. He asked me to understand, but I didn't. I was the one who broke it off when I wrote to him. I thought that was what he wanted."

Mrs. Luddington shook her head. "These dear John letters are bad business, Shelley. If they aren't righted, and quickly, they can lead to a lot of trouble. It's a pretty good idea not to mail a letter like that until you've had a chance to think it over."

"I haven't heard from him," Shelley said, her heart sinking even lower.

"If I know Arlan," Mrs. Luddington suggested after a little thought, "he won't let a letter stand in his way. What I'm afraid of is that he won't let the Coast Guard stand in his way either. He's very apt to drop everything and come right home here to fix things up. I just hope he doesn't chuck the Coast Guard, now that he's in it, go AWOL or something."

"Oh, he can't!" Shelley cried. "He mustn't! Oh . . ." She started up from her chair.

"Just a minute, Shelley," Mrs. Luddington said.

"First things first. We'll come to Arlan in due time. There are such things as telephones, you know. But I need to work on your other problem right now."

"It isn't just the money," Shelley explained, sinking a little reluctantly back down in her chair. "I have Vernon's pension, I guess. For a while anyhow. But from now on, I have to take care of myself, and I don't suppose they'll let me live alone. I'd like to work at Phoebe Crandall's hotel. Only I don't see how I can ask her for a job because of Arlan and the Brocks." She looked up and said slowly, "Just the same, it makes more sense than anything else."

"I think it does, too. Independence for most of us means a job, Shelley. It's a good thing to learn that early and not end up like your mother. Phoebe's a practical person, and she'll be looking first of all for someone who can do the work. Arlan won't be her first consideration even if he is her favorite nephew. In any case she's very fond of you. We've had some conversations about you already." Mrs. Luddington smiled. "Shelley, I need to do some telephoning on your behalf. Do you want to go to class?"

"No," Shelley said. "I don't."

"Then why don't you go and sit out on the beach for a while? It's a lovely day, and I'll send Jane out for you when I want you."

Shelley walked out to the beach and found a spot out of sight of the school windows. She looked across the water to Sentinel Head, hump after lessening hump until it seemed to sink indistinctly into the sea. Although she could see a part of the beach from her house, she couldn't detect from here a single building on Sentinel Head. It was as if the place where she lived didn't exist.

Yet that was her home. She had known it since the first night of her coming, maybe even before that, before she'd even known about Sentinel Head at all. In the end, having found it, she'd refused to leave. It had become a part of her.

Home was a place, a community, a family, even if the family wasn't your own. But home had to be more than that, because even if you lost all these things, you still knew where you belonged. Home was your deepest belonging, the direction and center of your life. You could spend a lifetime searching and never find your true home; she was lucky.

Sentinel Head was her home, but it wasn't Catherine's. The collision would have come sooner or later.

The incoming combers were breaking in ranks of five, and the music of the long surf soothed her as if its business were to heal. She'd lost Vernon and Catherine, perhaps Arlan, and she would probably have to leave Sentinel Head. But her feelings were right; this was home.

She saw the secretary come out of the building and start to cross the road to the beach. Shelley stood up and walked back into the building with her.

"Well," Mrs. Luddington said cheerfully when Shelley was again seated in the chair opposite her. "You're to go to Phoebe. It's all settled, and with two simple words, 'Of course.' She's getting in touch with her sister, and she's sure the Brocks will want to come right home." The last tight strings inside Shelley snapped, and she turned her head aside, trying not to cry.

"I'm sorry. I guess I've been awfully scared," she confessed. "I honestly don't bawl like this all the time."

"Of course you've been scared. Who wouldn't be?" Mrs. Luddington responded.

"Mrs. Luddington, I have to tell you," Shelley said, her voice still shaky, "I've really made an awful mess of things. I was supposed to take care of Catherine. I promised my father I would. He'd always said there were limits to what I could do, but just before he died, he . . ." Shelley bit her lip.

"Deathbed promises have caused a lot of mischief over the years," Mrs. Luddington observed. "People sometimes become childish toward the end, you know. It's not a good time for binding promises."

"I suppose he didn't mean to . . . make it impossible for me," Shelley said slowly. "The trouble was, I didn't know *how* to handle Catherine."

"Did he?" Mrs. Luddington asked gently. Shelley shook her head.

"Not really. He sort of gave up on her, before he died. I tried, though, until . . ."

There was a long silence. It went on for years, it seemed, while Shelley looked at the floor, but finally Mrs. Luddington asked, "Until?"

"I told Catherine to get out of my life and stay out of it. I did it on purpose—I mean, I meant it when I said it, and she knew I did. It was a terrible thing to do."

"Are you sure your mother hadn't been waiting for just some moment like that to give her an excuse to break away?" Mrs. Luddington suggested. Shelley felt a shock go through her entire system.

"But I thought Janet said I was expecting too much of her. She wasn't really a mother. I know that now, and I kept trying to push her into being one."

"Well, Shelley—perhaps." Mrs. Luddington looked thoughtful. "Suppose you turn it around. What's so terrible about a child expecting her mother to *be* a mother?"

"But I kept expecting her to be a *super* mother. She must have hated me for it," Shelley persisted.

"Oh?" Mrs. Luddington laughed, a deep, comfortable chuckle. "My own children keep telling me I don't live up to expectations, and I don't love them any the less."

Mrs. Luddington picked up her pen and looked at it thoughtfully. "I understand your mother's unhappiness, of course, and if you can, it will take some of the sting out of your memories. However, I don't go along with parents' abandoning their children, at any age."

"Arlan told me once Catherine would never get between us. But she did," Shelley said. "I let her come between us myself."

"Your feelings about your mother came between the two of you," Mrs. Luddington suggested. "All that anger, resentment, and guilt. No one's blaming you, Shelley."

"Just the same, Catherine must have felt the same way about me. After she met Roy Manning, she didn't want me hanging around. Like a mother." Why couldn't she keep her voice from shaking? Shelley wondered.

"It was never intended that the child should be the parent and the parent the child," Mrs. Luddington pointed out. "Sooner or later, you would have destroyed each other. She wouldn't have lasted here much longer anyway, I suspect, and she might have tried to uproot you as well."

"She did try. But I wouldn't leave."

"A lot of courage went into that decision. Well!" Mrs. Luddington said matter-of-factly. "Phoebe's absolutely delighted to have you. There will be legalities, of course. You'll be a ward of the court if your mother doesn't come back."

"She doesn't want to be tracked down," Shelley said. "She said she wasn't coming back, no matter what."

"The court will rely very heavily on recommendations from the community, meaning me and the Brocks. We'll keep you here, within hailing distance, anyhow, of Sentinel Head. Phoebe will see that you finish school, and I think you'll enjoy the work."

Shelley didn't answer. She was going to enjoy working at the hotel. Why was she still so sad?

"I have one more thing I want to say to you, Shelley." Mrs. Luddington's voice was grave, and Shelley looked up quickly.

"You've been a good daughter to your parents," she said firmly. "Your father would have been proud of you. You've done all anyone could have done and more. Don't be so hard on yourself." Mrs. Luddington pushed back her chair and got to her feet.

"You've been really nice to me," Shelley said, standing up and reaching for her backpack. "Thank you. I guess I'll always wish I had done better with Catherine, though. I keep thinking she painted my room. Even if it was mostly for Axel."

Mrs. Luddington walked over and took Shelley's hands. "Let your mother go," she said.

Shelley blinked back tears and tried to understand why letting Catherine go should have caused them. "I've decided to go to Halifax for the day," she said huskily. "I'm going to the Coast Guard base and find Arlan."

"Don't do that, Shelley," Mrs. Luddington said quickly. "A lonely girl combing the base for her boyfriend isn't going to work. He probably wouldn't even be able to see you. Wait until the Brocks get home this evening and call him."

"I've got to go somewhere," Shelley said desperately. "I have to think."

"Go on into Halifax anyway," Mrs. Luddington suggested. "It's a good idea to get away. Walk on down to the harbour and think there. I assume you're taking the bus? You have just time enough to catch it." Then she laughed. "This is the day for Halifax. I met Jaimie Wenlock, dressed fit to kill, on his way there this morning."

"Old Jaimie? I told him about Arlan and me last night. He was really upset," Shelley said slowly.

"I think, then, you may have a friend at court, Shelley. He told me he had business with the Coast Guard. It didn't occur to me it was Arlan." She smiled. "So you've picked up a grandfather along the way, have you?"

Old Jaimie

After taking Shelley home, Jaimie had driven back to Port Huyett in distress and some anger. He hadn't known how to help, and he ought to have done better. What the woman thought she was doing, running off and leaving a girl like that, he couldn't imagine. It would be good riddance, he thought, if it hadn't been for Shelley. He hoped she wouldn't have to leave now that she'd settled in. He hated to see Arlan and Shelley break up. He wondered impatiently what had come between the two of them. Some fool thing. Young people had no sense at all.

His telephone was ringing when he got home. The contraption had belonged to his wife, and he almost never used it. It almost never rang anymore in any case.

"Hello?" he growled into it. It was Axel Brock, calling from his cousin's place in the Valley, and he sounded well fashed. Arlan had just called from the base. He'd had a letter from Shelley. They wouldn't give him leave to come home, and he was threatening to go AWOL. It would mean the end of the Coast Guard for him.

"Tell him to hold his friggin' horses!" Jaimie yelled into the telephone, raising his voice to com-

pensate for the distance between himself and Axel.

Jaimie listened as Axel explained that he'd tried to talk to someone at the base, but he couldn't get anywhere on the phone. He didn't know anything about the Coast Guard. But he thought Jaimie with his years in the navy might know how to get through.

"Some damn O.D." Jaimie yelled.

"What?" asked Axel. Axel was a babe in the woods when it came to the military.

"Shelley's mother's pulled out and left her," Jaimie shouted. "Today." Jaimie could hear Axel begin to talk to Dru in the background.

"We'll be home tomorrow," Axel said finally. "Is Shelley all right"

Jaimie didn't know how to answer. How did he know whether Shelley was all right? "Got Arlan on her mind," he roared.

"Jaimie, is there any way we can get Arlan sprung for a couple days, do you think?" Axel asked.

Jaimie shouted that he'd think about it, and slamming the receiver back on its hook, he sat down to do so.

What was the friggin' hurry? he thought in irritation. Arlan would be getting leave soon, and he and Shelley could patch up whatever was wrong between them. Just the same, Arlan was stubborn as they came. He'd give up the Coast Guard in a minute if he made up his mind to it.

Jaimie sighed. He didn't want to, but his thoughts kept folding backward in spite of himself, the weight of his life was too heavy to stay balanced in the present, much less the future. He'd come close to *AWOL* himself once, in the months of hospital after the torpedoing. He'd sent Maiz a bitter letter—he'd completely forgotten the problem—but he'd gotten a Dear John letter in return. They wouldn't give him leave, and he'd appealed in desperation to the base chaplain. Maiz and he had had nigh fifty year of marriage.

Shelley had lots of gimp. He was grateful to her for pitching in and giving him a hand, as she so often did, and he'd liked her from the beginning. She'd make a good wife for Arlan. And Martin Brock and Conrad Joyner, his old comrades, had to be considered. Neither of them had had a chance to round out their lives. There was a lot of unfinished business for both of them.

Jaimie got up early the next morning and put on his best and only suit. At the last moment he opened his top dresser drawer, took out the box that held his old war medals. He looked at them for a moment and put the box back in the drawer. The old Royal Navy was his service, and everything was changed since his time. Except the military itself. That would be the same. He left Port Huyett a good hour before Shelley got there on the school bus, but he ran into Mrs. Luddington. Feeling the need to explain his suit, he'd blurted out to her that he was going to Halifax and something about the Coast Guard.

Several hours later, having arrived at the base and in the wake of more than a few startled faces, he brushed past a young girl decked out like a man in uniform and stood before the desk of Capt. James Argylle, post chaplain. Jaimie rapped with his knuckles on the desk, and the chaplain looked up, a questioning interest replacing his initial annoyance.

"I've come on a matter of impending desertion," Jaimie said gruffly. After all these years the whole damn military owed him something, an audience at least. He looked at the man sitting there, receptive and smiling a little, and it took him back to that other time. "Sir," he added with a stiffened salute. The chaplain pushed back his chair, stood up, and returned the salute.

Later, wryly satisfied with his mission, Jaimie drove from the base into the heart of the city. It had been a long time since he'd been there, though Halifax had been his home port during the war and he'd spent months in the city, hospitalized and later convalescent. He drove down to the harbour and parked the truck. Nothing looked familiar; he could have been in a foreign land. He walked through some fool tourist area to the water and stood on the wharf, gazing with interest and some wistfulness at the Bluenose II, the historic schooner moored there. He'd like the feel of a deck under his feet once more.

Chapter 19

SHELLEY WALKED FROM THE HALIFAX BUS STATION to the harbour, down the short, steep streets toward the sparkling water. It was breezy, there was always wind in Halifax, and it was a sunny spring day as well. Her spirits lifted.

All kinds of industry lined the harbour, buildings and water towers, gas tanks, warehouses facing it, some fancy hotels overlooking it, and wharves with workboats tied up to them. A little way up the harbour, Shelley could see a collection of old buildings and people milling around. The kids at school had talked about the Historic Properties, and she headed in that direction, following the harbour shore. Around a hub of old buildings, she reached the tourist area. It was overwhelming, a confusion of people, shops, venders, ice cream stands, motor launches, and tour boats. Shelley watched a ferry cutting diagonally across the harbour and longed to be on it, just to escape, to go anywhere at all.

Then she saw the schooner tied up to the wharf, and it reached out to her. She walked dreamily toward it, almost in a trance. She'd never imagined a more beautiful boat. Its masts and rigging rocked with the waves, metal clapped against wood, rope strained and creaked. People were aboard, working with the gear. The *Bluenose II*, Lunenburg, and you could go out in her, under sail, for a trip in the harbour.

An old man stood at the edge of the wharf, looking over the ship.

"Let's go out in her, Jaimie," Shelley said gently.

He must be getting used to her, she thought; he didn't look in the least thunderstruck. He only gave a grunt of assent and then waved her away when she fished in her bag for ticket money. They walked up the gangplank, climbed aboard, and sat on a low bench alongside the rail, side by side. Shelley looked up and saw that the rigging broke the brilliant, blue sky above her into patterns.

They sailed out into the harbour by motor, perhaps farther than usual because of the lovely May day. Shelley turned once to check out Old Jaimie, but seeing the look on his face, she thought maybe he had forgotten all about her. She blocked out the sight of the other passengers, shut out their chatter from her ears. She was scarcely aware of the tourist guide indicating points of interest along the shores, explaining the facts of the great World War I explosion in the harbour, showing where the devastation had occurred and on and on. The schooner finally slowed and turned back toward port. The crew worked with the ropes, and presently the sails loosened. While Shelley held her breath, they ran upward, caught the wind and filled. The motor stopped its thrumming, the guide his patter, and they skimmed silently over the water, only the ropes straining as if their muscles were flexing in a joyous bit of exercise.

And freedom. Shelley looked upward at the blinding white of the sails against the blue spring sky. The wind rushed past her, the schooner caught up with the swells coming in from the ocean and cut into them. For the first time in her whole life she was free, like the schooner, bound to nothing but air and water, and she could go where she liked. The responsibility that had imprisoned her to Catherine all these years softened. "Let your mother go," Sarah Luddington had said. It was as if she had released Shelley into the glory of sail. They were riding noiselessly before the wind, and Shelley, breaking all ties with the earthbound, *became* the schooner, a lifetime of care streaking backward from her as the boat thrust through the water.

As the schooner docked, Shelley turned once more to check Jaimie and quickly looked away. She didn't know what she had read in his face, but whatever it was, it was too much his for her to interfere. It had to do with contentment, though, and peace, and she thought he was entitled to them. They had found what they had come for, both of them; nothing else was needed. They walked back to the parking lot and the truck, and Old Jaimie drove Shelley home to Sentinel Head.

Shelley learned from Axel, not Jaimie, the details of Jaimie's trip to Halifax and the outcome of it, a weekend pass for Arlan. He'd be home on Saturday. For two whole days!

"Time for you two idiots to settle your differences," growled Axel. "A proper mess the two of you got yourselves into." There was a lot more scolding, and then Shelley had to weather Dru's distress at losing her, even to Phoebe.

"Just when I know that Sentinel Head is really home, I have to leave it." Shelley sighed. She was comfortable, sitting at the Brocks' table, secure. It was hard to lose it all.

"You don't leave Sentinel Head," Axel said seriously. "You just go away for a little while."

Shelley nodded. She already knew.

Until the weekend and Arlan's pass, Shelley packed and made her house ready for the rapturous Janet and grateful Craig, who were going to live in it. She had steeled herself to cleaning up after Catherine, but there was nothing to do. The room was bare of her, as if she had never occupied it; not a shred of Catherine remained. Janet and Craig, by living there, would soften the place, though, and Vernon's sad little room could be turned into a nursery for a new baby.

Sweeping the house clean of the Joyners was the least of her chores. There were farewells to be said, legalities to transact, interviews, and school transfers. On the morning that Arlan, in a borrowed truck, was due to arrive, Shelley, well behind schedule, was giving the kitchen floor a hasty last scrubbing. When Arlan burst through the kitchen door, that's where he found her, scrubbing, not at all glamorous. He hugged her, mop and all.

"Arlan, you look absolutely wonderful in that uniform!" Shelley told him, half laughing, half crying.

"I'm going to put you on a shelf, where I can look at you for the rest of my life."

She looked up at him, at the seriousness in his face. In the end Catherine had not come between them, not any more than the floor mop. In this little time life had unfolded for both of them, and whatever the earlier hurt, it was no longer important. They wouldn't need even to mention the letters. Laying aside the mop, Shelley returned to Arlan's arms. There wasn't "always the telephone," as Mrs. Luddington had said. Sometimes you had to see. And feel. She laid her head into Arlan's shoulder.

"We aren't either of us going to sit on a shelf," Arlan said after a moment. "We've got a whole life together." Shelley looked up at him and watched him slowly smile, as if their future were dawning at the same time. "Come on, Shelley, I'll give you a hand here," he said briskly. "I'm getting a lot of practice with mops, and then let's walk out on the Head. Mum's cooking up a big dinner for us, but we have a little while."

The lovely weekend was coming to a close. Arlan was to drive Shelley to Spruce Point on his way back to the base. "There's one more thing I have to do before we leave," Shelley told him. "I want to walk down to the cemetery and plant this ivy. It's a last rite," she added. She picked up two of Catherine's plants and took a final look around the house. Everything was in order, and Janet and Craig could move in the next day.

"Do you want me to go with you?" Arlan asked. "That soil's hard to dig into."

"I want to do this one alone," Shelley answered. "Could you pick me up in half an hour? I'll be ready."

"I'll put your things in the truck, then, and go back and say good-bye to the folks." He smiled and kissed her. "It's time for you to say good-bye, too," he said.

Shelley walked the short distance to the graveyard, and let herself in the gate. The hardscrabble soil was more friable than she had expected, and she leaned back on her heels in satisfaction when she had finished. The green ivy softened the stark headstone and would last for the summer, anyhow.

Her anger was gone, and all that was left was sadness, just plain acceptance of what was and what had been. She started to cry. After all, grief wasn't such a terrible thing, and Vernon was deserving of it. She stood up finally, and wiping her eyes, she looked quietly down at the grave for a little while, until, as she had with Catherine, though more sweetly, she could let Vernon go too.

Shelley heard the truck pull up in the road. "Thanks for bringing me home, Vernon," she whispered. Then she slipped through the gate and, opening the truck door, climbed in beside Arlan.

The door slammed, the truck shifted gears, and drove off. The grind of the gravel died away, and in the graveyard no sound remained but the even roll of the sea.

Old Jaimie

On Sentinel Head summer had just settled in, and the tourists were back. The fishing fleet was out, and the house yards were full of garden flowers. Axel, on his way out to the Head, passed the Joyner house and smiled. Janet was a nest builder from way back, and already Shelley's windows were criss-crossed with priscillas. He was going to miss Shelley. The whole neighborhood would. Odd how she'd fitted right in. She'd be back someday, he hoped, though you could never tell with the young.

Axel climbed easily over the gate. He'd seen the truck go by, and he expected to find Jaimie somewhere out on the moor.

Jaimie was sitting on a rock far out on the headland, an unaccustomed indulgence for him. He was increasingly in poor health. He admitted it, and he thought there was not a great deal of sunlight remaining to him. He smiled briefly as Axel sat down beside him.

"I thought you'd like to know that Shelley's doing fine with Phoebe Crandall," Axel said.

Jaimie nodded.

"Arlan says they plan on getting married after his sea duty, about a year," Axel continued. "He wants Shelley to finish school. She'll stay with

Phoebe until Arlan gets a permanent base. She wants to go on working, says she doesn't like to sit around."
The two men sat looking seaward, companionable in their silence.
At last Jaimie said calmly, "I'm selling the sheep."
"Well," said Axel, "it's time. It's time. Each thing in its season." After a few more minutes he got up and strolled off down the cliff path, leaving Jaimie to his thoughts.
So it was starting all over. Old Jaimie found the idea pleasing. Conrad Joyner and Martin Brock. They'd had their season. Vernon and Axel in their generation. And now Arlan and Shelley. On the Head everything came back to its beginnings. One of these days there'd be a spring without him. He could accept that, but the circle would carry on, the sheep, the lambings, the seasons, the tides. At the roadside, in their turn, the flowers. He'd had a fondness for them, in the spring, the broom, the lupines, then the roses and daisies, the evening primrose, Saint-John's-wort, and late in the summer, the black-eyed Susan, the pearly everlasting.